Cover art by Bill Price.

This book is a work of fiction. Names, characters, places, and incidents either are products of the author's imagination or are used fictitiously. Any resemblance to actual persons, living or dead, events, or locales is entirely coincidental.

First Printing: July 2018
Amazon

Elaine
Thank you for buying my book
Love

# FOUR SEVEN TWO

Robert. A. Mitchell

*For my family and friends, especially those who stick by me when times are tough.*

# 1992

# Chapter 1

"FUCK FUCK FUCK!"

Detective Inspector Morris' voice boomed throughout Grimsby police station as he repeatedly slammed the phone against the base until it eventually fell off the desk. He'd just had some devastating news. Exceptionally bad. A third rape with exactly the same modus operandi which looked to have been perpetrated by the same person. Local park in the Grimsby/Cleethorpes area and not a lot to go by in the way of evidence or a description. 5'7 to 5'10 "ish" medium "ish" build and a black woollen balaclava. It looked like they'd have to admit it was a serial rapist and give in to the Evening Telegraph's moniker "The Beast in a Balaclava" and he resented that more than anything.

He grabbed his coat as he made his way out of the nick and got in his car for the drive to Grimsby Hospital. The car stereo was on a little too loud as Jimmy Nail blasted his ear drums. Morris punched the off button.

"I'll give you she's lying you fucking Geordie twat!" He screamed as he pulled onto Victoria Street and headed towards Scartho.

Meeting one of the uniformed officers outside the main hospital doors he lit a cigarette whilst being told the situation.

"She's in a bad way this one sir, really shook up but reckons she might be able to give us a good e-fit"

"Bollocks" thought Morris, how will it be better than the other 2 e-fits of a pair of nondescript eyes in a fucking balaclava?

Back in his car he made his way over to the crime scene to see what little evidence the team over there had managed to dig up. He wasn't surprised when he learnt absolutely none. No footprints, no eye witnesses, nothing to provide any DNA, just nothing. How the hell was he meant to catch him? Just how?

# 1997

# Chapter 2

Ben checked his watch, 6:05. It hadn't seemed like 10 minutes since the usual 2 o'clock proceedings of Walter Murphy's California Strut, bright lights, gamble whilst staggering down the stairs and stumble over to Victoria Kebab House for those who'd made the end of another night at Grimsby's premier (well realistically only) nightclub Gullivers. To the untrained; or at least "foreign"; eye this would seem a very odd sight as a mixture of Goths, greebos, metalheads, punks, skaters and wannabe mod/indie kids pile out of the same door which seemingly leads nowhere. Many of the different cultures intermingling and deep in conversation in friendships that to the outside world should not really work.

One such pairing Ben and Stu were as disparate as you could think. Ben an obvious mod in his parka and coiffured Weller style hair and Stu with his long hair and leather jacket were best of mates and had certainly been putting the world to rights tonight on that bench. No topic had been off limits and Stu was actually quite pleased Ben had stayed because he'd usually gone off with a girl by now.

"Right Stu, it's been a pleasure as always but I've got to go. Catching the bus to Fulham for the Town game"

"Seriously?"

"Yeah mate, I know, Tim goes to uni on Sunday so I promised him, what can you do?"

"You out Tuesday?"

"Yeah mate. Same time same place?"

Ben got up. Stu was right the football wasn't really him nowadays. Well the actual match was but the shenanigans of going with a group of yobbos on a bus and getting there for opening time was well out of his system.

But he and Tim were oldest mates. Born 2 days apart and lived next door but one to each other until they were 12 and Ben's mum and Dad split up. They'd kind of drifted apart since Tim went to Franklin and Ben decided to concentrate on his music too. Tim opting for the football violence, nights out in Meggies and the trappings and delights of that whereas Ben going out in Gy or staying in smoking dope. Anyway Tim had said Fulham's firm probably wouldn't show so not much chance of violence and they could just have a good old chinwag before Tim went away and hopefully come home with 3 points.

As he turned onto Welholme Road, he saw a guy he recognised from the football talking to a slightly overweight copper with a tache. They were talking quite jovially but in hushed tones. He overheard the copper joking with the guy whose name he didn't know

"Yeah just pulled him on the Nunny, I reckon about 5 or 6 ounces but of course that'll be 1 or 2 before we get him to the nick"

Ben made a mental note to find out this guy's name and befriend him to maybe try to procure some of this wayward merchandise.

The coach was already on the 'Sheaf car park by the time Ben got there so he climbed aboard and was greeted by a beaming Craig who it now appeared was the organiser of the "battle bus". Craig was about 5 foot 5 and 8 stone wet through but wasn't scared of anything or anyone.

"Well bugger me sideways young Benjamin"
"Alright Craig?"
"Too long a time no see. Young Timothy said you were coming, even paid your fare, but I wouldn't have believed it without my own eyes. Hope you're still a game little bastard, Millwall at home next week could do with you seeing as student boy's buggering off,"

Ben shrugged his shoulders and tried to crack a smile. He knew full well he had a gig in Nottingham next Saturday and he was only here because he felt a duty to Tim. He went over to where Tim and the rest of the lads were sat. He knew most of them but it appeared Karl, Tim's younger brother and a few of his mates had started coming. Introductions were made and Ben forgot names as quickly as he was told them. Ben looked to the door of the coach at exactly the wrong time as he saw Macca boarding. He wasn't sure if it was audible but he inwardly groaned. This meant a few things. firstly Tim's promise of little or no violence wasn't going to be withheld and secondly lots of topics of conversation were now out the window.

Steve "Macca" MacKenzie was the middle child and only boy of seven siblings. He was reasonably anonymous with mousy brown hair and of average height and weight yet he certainly made an impression in today's attire of a canary yellow Stone Island jacket. his borderline psychopathic behaviour was pretty much known about throughout the town and that he was not one to be messed with and he revelled in his reputation.

One of Ben and Tim's usual favourite games was ranking the six MacKenzie sisters in the order in which you'd shag them. For Ben this was really a choice of 2 because Hannah and Katie were jailbait and he'd already fucked Jodie and Clare; who he had noted were remarkably similar in bed. The other cause of much mirth amongst most lads their age, and probably beyond, was the noticeable hard-on of not so large proportion in Macca's jeans whenever he was having a scrap. This was made even funnier by the rumour spread by Steve; the landlord of the Jube on the estate; that he'd managed to pull one of the barmaids once but couldn't get it up and when she'd come downstairs had found him wanking. There were discrepancies in the story that he was either watching I.D. and wanking over Reece Dinsdale during the fight scenes or the balcony glassing scene in Trainspotting. Either way is that she'd watched him and it took less than a minute and his cock was small. Ben openly, and Tim secretly, doubted the story because of the discrepancy and the fact Macca clammed up whenever he spoke to a girl who wasn't his sister let alone manage to pull one plus neither of them had ever seen him drinking in the Jube since he moved from his mums to Meggies.

The coach turned out of the car park and a cacophony of cans opening, spliffs being lit and lines being sniffed greets left turn onto Bargate in a ritualistic choosing of today's poison by the followers of this odd cult. Craig bounds down the coach inspecting today's crew like a general inspecting their army. Passing comments about another coach from the tavern and a few cars of older school lads from the Valiant to anyone enquiring. He gets to Ben and Tim.

"So then uni boy, where is it you're going?"

Tim rather embarrassingly mutters Bradford. It wasn't his first choice, truth be told it wasn't his second third or fourth choice but they did the politics degree he wanted to do and they had him through clearing and so Bradford it was.

"Fuck me you'll either turn into a Yorkie or come back speaking Paki, stinking of curry and wearing a turban."

Ben bit his tongue as although he had an overwhelming urge to correct this racist diatribe of misinformation he had an even more overwhelming urge to not have his face smashed in before the sun had got over the yard arm.

Δ Δ Δ

As they arrived in London and find the pub that had been carefully selected and scrutinised by Craig last week Ben felt a relief that he could relax a little and not have to be so careful as to his choice of words or topics of conversation. The relaxation was complete by the cute little blonde behind the bar. Now Ben knew he wasn't the best looking lad in the world but for some reason he was very comfortable speaking to girls and had a talent for saying exactly the right things to get into their knickers which he used to great aplomb. He was always helped in this department by girls talking and therefore stories circulating of his 9 inches. Since losing his virginity at 14 Ben had never had a relationship yet the longest he'd been without sex was 3 weeks, at 18 he'd already lost count of the number of girls he'd bedded or taken a walk to People's Park with after gullies. Staying up all night and not relieving his balls, coupled with an alcohol buzz from last night topped up on the coach and a cute barmaid suddenly got Ben a little horny and he decided that the barmaid was going to be the latest girl in an ever increasing list to succumb to his charms.

"I'll get this round lads."

Jessica checked that the disabled toilet was empty and beckoned Ben over. She locked the door, and they kissed awkwardly both going the same way at first then locking in with passion. Ben lifted her skirt up and started teasing her clit, she was pretty wet already so he slid 2 fingers in and fed the horse exactly how they used to discuss on the school bus after reading his elder sister's Cosmopolitan article on G-spots. Her hand frantically undoing his belt and flies and she comments on his size as she teases him to hardness. Ben grabs her and turns her around pushes her against the wall and rips her panties to one side as he slides his cock deep into her in one go. Her moans are adequately muffled by Ben's hand over her mouth as he works his magic behind her. He feels her pussy start to contract against his big hard cock as her orgasm builds up inside her...

"Yes yes."
"YESSSSSSSS!"

Macca's voice puts Ben off his rhythm as he hears tables being turned over and glasses smashing. His balls still not empty he buttons up his jeans and steadies himself for the scenes of chaos that await him as he opens the door. “Fucking hell” he thought to himself.

∆ ∆ ∆

Those who decided to go to Craven Cottage and not stay in the pub or get themselves arrested witnessed a Steve Livingstone brace as Town ran out 2-0 winners. On the coach on the way home a tune came into Ben’s head, he closed his eyes and wished he had his guitar in his hands. Not that these Neanderthal bastards would appreciate it. He dozed off thinking to himself he must work harder with his music and hearing the generic Northern accents talking rubbish about the day’s events reaffirmed in his head that in order to get somewhere he must move out of Grimsby, and pretty damn sharpish.

# Chapter 3

Hannah MacKenzie's head was firmly on her shoulders and her behaviour and thought process far in advance of her nearly 14 years on this planet. In part it was down to having five elder sisters and was helped by her early onset of puberty meaning by the time she was 11 she had D cup boobs and was therefore treat as an adult by everyone around her.

She was talking, well listening, to Gemma on the 'phone as she recounted the story of her "skiing" with two guys on the school field after youth club the other night. Gemma, like Hannah, was advanced for her age but didn't have Hannah's cool demeanour around guys and just couldn't help herself. In other words she was a slag and pretty much everyone at school and on the estate knew this. Hannah grew bored of her story very quickly and was only really picking up the odd word here and there but typically of Gemma those words were pretty much "cocks", "wanking" and "cum". Hannah let out a smug smile as she commended herself on not telling Gemma everything and was pleased everyone, including her closest sister Katie, thought she was still a virgin.

Hannah's mind wandered to her boyfriend. Well lover. He'd not officially asked her out and they'd only shagged four times so she wasn't sure if she could class him as a boyfriend or not. Besides he was 18 and just gone off to uni so there probably wasn't much of a chance of it ever becoming serious anyway. Plus he'd clarified that her brother Steven was never to find out about them so there wasn't much chance of him taking her into town or down Meggies holding hands. But God, she missed him.

Why did Steven have to be like he was? There was times she was glad of his protection but it would have been nice to actually be able to speak to boys without knowing if they were only being nice because of Steven or they were avoiding her for the exact same reason. At least it wasn't just her; he was like it with all six of them, even the elder sisters who in reality should have been looking out for him. She recollected a story of a guy Jodie liked who'd eventually built up the balls to ask her out and how Steven had "had a word" which resulted in a broken nose and a barrage of kicks to the poor lad's nether regions which had split his scrotum and ruptured one of his testicles and had; if rumour were to be believed; rendered him no longer able to sire children.

The conversation with Gemma had ended and she's put the phone back on the receiver without really paying any attention to the end of the conversation - had she even said goodbye? She laid back and cuddled the teddy he'd bought her before he'd gone as a solitary tear ran down her cheek which then turned into uncontrollable sobs as she convinced herself that she had probably been used this summer and had let him coerce her into giving not only her vaginal, but her anal virginity too, with his charms. She wished that her life could be simpler, probably more like Gemma's but without the constant fear of getting up the duff or the clap and certainly not the reputation of being the Willow's bike. She cried and cried until eventually she fell asleep even though it was only early evening on a Sunday.

She awoke on Monday morning still teary and now with the added stress that she hadn't done her Maths homework. She decided to take the 45 instead of the official school bus and do it on there on the short trip to Healing. Besides she couldn't be arsed listening to the story of Gemma's night from the two guys she wanked off at the same time anyway.

# Chapter 4

Somewhere in between a state of consciousness and sleep Tim felt a deep pressure on his chest. In his dream this was finally it, the end. He'd dreamt of dying before but this time he knew it was different. This time he was sure. He was struggling to breathe, the pressure in his chest getting heavier and heavier, like something double his body weight was pressing on his rib cage. He couldn't move his arms, they were forcibly attached to his side. A vice tightened around his throat and he could taste blood and then a sharp pain in his nose, and again, and again, and.....

He woke with a start to see Macca straddling him knees pinning his arms to his side. Faces so close he could practically taste the saliva hissing out of Macca's mouth and smell a heady mixture of halitosis, Embassy Number 1, weed and Carlsberg as he snarled.

“Macca what the fuck?”

“Don’t even try fucking denying it you fucking cunt”

“Wha. Wha. What the fuck?”

Tim tried to swing an arm up to clock him or at least push him off. He knew that wasn’t the wisest move with Macca’s penchant for hospitalising people but he was going one way or another and he sure as hell wasn’t going down without a fight and needed to give himself a sporting chance.

“My fucking kid sister”

“What?”

“She’s fucking 13 you fucking nonce. I’m gonna fucking enjoy cutting your fucking bollocks off. I’m gonna do you nice and fucking slowly you fucking cunt”

Shit, Tim thought, how the fuck did he find out? He contemplated lying but could tell Macca knew the truth. Well half the truth and Tim wasn’t sure telling him that at first he thought it was Katie the 16 year old sister and not Hannah would placate this situation any further. Especially when it had happened more than once.

"But but"

"Fuck off cunt!"

Macca rained 6 or 7 head-butts onto the bridge of Tim's now practically non-existent nose and Tim was struggling to breathe again. The pressure in his chest relieved for a second as Macca reached behind his back to pull the knife from his belt. Tim knew this was it, the pressure building up in his chest again and the vice-like grip getting stronger around his throat. Macca lunged forward......

He woke with a start dripping in sweat and crying. His eyes adjusting to the mixture of tears and darkness and adrenaline pumping ready for a fight he focussed on the red numbers of the alarm clock.

4:17

"Fuck man, fuck....." he said to nobody in particular, he needed a smoke so carefully stood up to place the sock over the smoke detector. Some dickhead at the uni had placed him in non-smoking halls and he sure as hell wasn't going outside in the pissing down rain. They'd only been at uni a day when the Manc guy, Ian, opposite had worked out you could circumvent the detectors with a sock, carrier bag and elastic band. He grabbed the golden packet of Benson and Hedges off the desk, hands still shaking like an epileptic Parkinson's alcoholic before his first can of the day. "Fuck" none left.

Fortunately there was half a spliff left in the ashtray so he sparked it up and took a deep inhale. His lungs burned as the nasty resin hit his system. He held it in there probably a bit longer than he should because no smoke came out when he exhaled but it had the desired effect of calming him down yet his mind was going ten to the dozen.

Once he'd finished he stubbed the spliff out and went over to the sink that was inexplicably in every room in this halls of residence. He washed his face three times then had a piss in the sink before retiring back to his barely the same size as him bed.

His mind drifted to Hannah. Yes she was young and yes he was sure he'd been her first but she had great tits and knew how to empty his bollocks. She was also pretty cool and knew her music and had a pretty smile. Fucking hell, did he love her? Her tits came quickly back into his mind and he thought about having a wank but an image of Macca came into his head equally as quick and dissipated any sign of an erection he had brewing.

He laughed. That's all you could really do in this situation. Laugh.

First thing tomorrow, he thought, was work out if Ian knew where to buy some decent weed from in this Yorkshire shithole and possibly something a bit more weekend related, but more importantly, much more importantly, make sure no-one, absolutely no-one, especially Macca finds out about him and Hannah's summer.

# Chapter 5

Karl stood and let the hot water trickle over the back of his neck, he looked down at his cock and pulled his foreskin back. He used his pubes to lather up the shower gel to a big foam before rubbing it up his stomach and chest. He tapped his gut and thought he really needed to cut back on the ale as a beer belly on a 16 year old was neither healthy nor attractive. He thought about the weekend's events and let out a wry smile followed by an overwhelming urge to cry. They'd given Tim a good sendoff but now he'd gone to Bradford to study and Karl was pretty much stuck at home on his own now to deal with his Dad whenever he came round pissed kicking off with his Mum and Ray. Karl liked Ray but the guy was a bit of a faggot when it came to defending his wife and home.

Buttoning up his shirt and tightening his tie he glanced in the mirror just to make sure he looked as good as he could and quickly went next door into Tim's room to look in his wardrobe. "Fucking get in" he thought as he noticed Tim had left his new Henri Lloyd black label jacket quickly grabbing it and trying it on for size "I'm having this bastard". He ran downstairs and nodded at Ray, grabbed some toast and kissing his Mum before bounding out the door to make his way to school.

"Bollocks!" He exclaimed loudly as he got to the corner of Priory Road and St Nicholas Drive as he realised there was nobody else at the bus stop. It wasn't too much of an issue as the bus did the mile loop round the estate before heading off and up Great Coates Road to Healing. He turned on his heel to make his way up past the Jube to catch it on Wybers Way on its way off. About 100 yards away from the roundabout he noticed the bus was already stopped where he was going to catch it so he upped his pace to bounding then an eventual run as the bus pulled off. Martin was knocking on the window grinning like a Cheshire Cat giving him the wanker wave.

"Fuck it! Bastard!"

Well his day could only get better now he thought and much better he thought as he walked down to get the 45 and saw a very familiar shape at the bus stop. Hannah had been his go to wank for the past few months and he'd recognise her arse anywhere.

"Alright Han?" he shouted almost too enthusiastically before he'd properly got to the bus stop.

"Hey Karlos the Jackal" she said, happy to see him as she knew she know had someone who could do her homework without too much effort from herself.

They made their way upstairs and she turned on the charm in order to get him to do her work. She kind of felt a pang of guilt prickteasing him now that her and Tim were whatever they were. She knew Karl fancied her but she also knew he idolised Tim. He sat there smoking his fag telling her what the answers were.

"You gonna give us a drag on that or what?"

He tapped the ash on the floor and passed it over to her hoping she didn't notice him staring for probably too long at her Wonderbra enclosed tits which were accentuated by the bra being black under her white shirt. His mind wandered to his default wank fantasy with her about what it would be like to get his cock between her tits and he felt an erection building up. He adjusted himself on the chair to try and settle it down and so that it wouldn't be noticed and tried to re-concentrate on her Maths and not his fantasy about the tit wank. After all, a fantasy was all it would ever be. Firstly she was 13 and only in year 9 while he was already 16 and in year 11 and secondly, and probably most importantly she was a MacKenzie and he was probably only getting away with talking because he was part of the "youth" and Tim's brother.

They were met off the bus by Hannah's mate Gemma who Karl was probably the only lad at school who hadn't been there. They shared a fag between the three of them and chatted about nothing. The bell signalling the start of their school day rang out loud and they made their separate ways with Karl having to run up the "down" stairs to get to registration on time to avoid another unnecessary bollocking.

Martin and the others were all clearly stoned and giggling like little girls to themselves and from what Karl could make out Riles had invented some sort of new pipe out of a Remington "Fuzzaway" and it had hit them hard. That was the best reason to befriend Riles, he was always coming up with newer technological methods to further advance the enablement of getting stoned.

"He's got an idea" said Martin
"Oh yeah?"
"Yeah he just needs to liberate his mam's hoover"
"Fuck sake"

∆ ∆ ∆

At lunch time they crossed over the road to the little copse of trees that had become their regular haunt. He had thought about inviting Hannah but the "MacKenzie Factor" had come into play and he wasn't so sure inviting the youngest sister for a smoke was the best way to avoid any form of fractured bones. He also didn't really know Hannah's views on drug use so thought that keeping it on the down low for the while might enhance the chances of getting his dick wet.

Riles pulled out the now infamous Fuzzaway and started the battery, he carefully lit the weed on the gauze and Karl marvelled as the plumes of blue smoke were drawn into the compartment that Victor Kayam had intended for little bits of fluff attached to posh people's clothes. Riles took a hit and then passed the device to Karl with a "be careful" look on his face. Riles, while an absolute stoner, was always the considerate one and made sure his friends were ok. He was the one they bought all their gear off. He wasn't a dealer per se, and he wasn't even one of these lads who dealt to mates to make a bit on the side to cover his own use. He dealt to them out of genuine concern that actual dealers may push harder stuff onto his mates and he didn't want to see his mates turn into to dirty smackheads. It even went as far as any wholesale bulk discount he managed to be privy to was passed directly to mates and if he'd been lucky enough to get an overweigh then this was distributed fairly and evenly also.

Karl placed the weed on the area designed for placing against the clothes which was now covered in a homemade kitchen foil gauze , sparked his lighter and turned on the device. He held it up to his mouth and he took an elongated inhale of the contents. It hit him harder than he anticipated and his lungs were on fire followed quickly by palpitations and a struggle to focus on what was around him. Feeling his countenance lighten as the blood left his face and his auditory response dull very quickly so that he couldn't hear the guffaws of his friends and the comments that White was quite an appropriate surname for him at the moment. His stomach tensed and he felt the acid rising up to his throat as his stomach contents splashed out onto the muddy floor.

After he had eventually finished laughing, Riles and Martin took pity on their incapacitated friend and slowly fed him Mars bar to help cure the whitey by upping his sugar levels. A technique Martin's well-travelled cousin had apparently learned in India and had passed on the knowledge. Eventually Karl was able to talk.

"Fuck me Riles that's good"

"I know Whitey, maybe be a bit less eager next time?"

Whatever the future without Tim held Karl knew one thing and that, thanks to Riles help, was he was going to be stoned for a considerable portion of it.

# Chapter 6

Vikki didn't know if she was looking forward to tonight or not. For a start she knew that she didn't look old enough to drink and it would be a pain having to produce her passport every time she wanted a vodka. The other thing was, even though she had lived there all her life, she had never actually been out drinking in Grimsby before. At school she had been a shy girl and not really had the types of friends that chanced going out drinking and she's kept the same friends into Franklin but had decided she really must concentrate on getting her grades if she wanted to become a nurse like she had always dreamed of so nights out were few and far between especially after having to resist her English GCSE. She still didn't quite know how she managed an E first time round yet an A* on resit. The few nights she had had out were either to the Harvest Moon in the village for quiz night or a student union do up in Cleethorpes.

Tonight was her cousin Suzi's hen do and they were going out in Grimsby on a pub crawl and then going to Gullivers. Despite never having been in any of the places Vikki had already decided that they weren't the kind of place for her but resigned herself to the fact that it had been nice for Suzi to ask plus she could always escape when her Auntie Jackie decided it was time to leave the young ones to it. Vikki liked Suzi, she was a few years older but had really become a rock for her when her Mum had passed away and had helped buy her first bra and helped her when her periods started talking her through and buying her Tampax and stuff. Suzi was a bit more rock chick, almost Goth, than Vikki and her mainstream poppy friends so they'd kind of drifted apart after Vikki had transcended from adolescence to young adulthood. In spite of her trepidation about the choice of venues, Vikki had jumped at the chance to spend the night with Suzi and Auntie Jackie, her Mum's sister, and was kind of pleased that they'd thought of her.

Vikki's Dad was sat in his chair reading the evening's Sports Telegraph. The Mighty Mariner was happy so she knew Town had won. She started reminiscing of when her Dad used to take her down to Blundell Park but had stopped after a rather unsavoury scene on Harrington Street when he wasn't sure he could protect her fully. He raised his eyes from the paper.

"Ant you better start getting ready?"

"There's loads of time yet Dad"

"Hardly, it takes you yonks to put your war paint on"

"Ok Dad, I'll go in a minute. Did Auntie Jackie say where to meet them?"

"The ring of feathers"

Vikki, unwittingly and somewhat naively walked straight into the gag her Dad had set her up for and walked upstairs shaking her head smiling as her Dad kept repeating "round a duck's arse" over and over. She opened her wardrobe and wondered what the hell to wear. She didn't want to look too poppy or overdressed, nor did she want to look like she'd made too much effort. She decided an outfit of all black might be overdoing it so opted for a flowery Miss

Selfridge top, a black denim skirt, tights and knee high leather boots. She had no idea why but whilst in the shower she decided to tidy up her pubic area after shaving her legs. Looking in the mirror she decided to leave her strawberry blonde hair down for the evening. She gazed at her thin body and barely existent breasts and she decided tonight was definitely a padded Wonderbra night.

∆ ∆ ∆

Upstairs in Chambers the raucousness and cackling of girl's laughter was almost unbearable to Vikki as the stripper covered his cock in squirty cream out of a can. Vikki wasn't what you'd called experienced but was by no means an angel either. She had seen precisely 3 penises in her life and although she knew this wasn't a lot, and although the stripper wasn't erect she was mightily impressed by his length and girth. The screams grew louder as the stripper forced Suzi to lick the cream off. In spite of her initial reservations, Vikki was having a fun night and was buoyed, and slightly heady, from the jugs of "Italian Job" cocktails which seemed to be in endless supply and seemed to taste a lot better when sent over from a group of lads all wearing Fred Perrys and Liam Gallagher hairdos, the ringleader of whom; a guy identified as Trigger who she recognised from Franklin; was seemingly going round the table declaring which one of the girls he would bed. Although embarrassed she was quite pleased to overhear him declare her as a "yes" and had to stifle a giggle when she heard him declare Auntie Jackie as "old, but yeah I would she's got great barns".

∆ ∆ ∆

It was true, time does fly when you're having fun and Vikki gave no signs of a fight as she found herself climbing the stairs to "Gullies" arms linked with Suzi like age old friends. Suzi proclaiming to the girl at the entrance-cum-cloakroom "one member and one Gullies virgin please." The large dark bouncer smiled at Vikki and she thought "Fuck he's gonna ID me and I've not brought my passport" but instead he opened the mirrored door for them. Vikki looked in awe as she saw a mirrored dance floor in front of her through the smoke and lots of little nooks and crannies full of people of all types of genre sat chatting. Suzi turned right and went up three steps to one such area and parked herself in one of the corners behind a table. The big bouncer came over with a beaming smile.

"Hen do Suzi?"

"Whatever gave you that idea Chris?" She said whilst puffing up her net curtain veil and swinging her obligatory "L" plate necklace.

"And who's the Gullies virgin?"

"Me cousin Vikki. Vikki - Chris"

"Eh up Vikki here's some champagne for you"

He plonked a bottle, but no glasses, down on the table and motioned for Vikki to drink. She looked at the bottle quizzically and noticed "Bucks Fizz" on the label so took it to her mouth and gulped. It was possibly the worst thing she'd ever tasted. Acid building up in her stomach as it ran down her gullet like bleach.

"Where's the loo Suze?"

"Just down there past the dance floor. I'll come with you in case you get lost and I'll go to the bar on the way back. Vodka and coke?"

Vikki was unsure if Suzi was being genuine or taking the piss. The dance floor was less than 10 metres long, some steps another less than 10 metre stretch past some tables then the toilet door. As she passed the bank of tables she noticed Ben talking animatedly to a long haired guy she knew from the chippy near college. Vikki always had had a soft spot for Ben at school but never acted on it for fear of rejection and she'd been told he only liked older women.

Ben paused briefly from his inane conversation with Stu to admire the strawberry blonde who'd just walked past. He barely recognised her at first and had to wrack his brain before it eventually clicked. For the next hour he silently watched like a lioness assessing her prey. He recognised the Goth girl in a net curtain veil she was talking to as well and decided that it was probably best to try and avoid a three way conversation. Eventually an extended period of rock was playing and Vikki was alone. He gave Stu the look that Stu had seen numerous times before, winked

"Wish me luck Stu"
"Like you bloody need it. Tuesday?"
"Same time same place"

He took the longer way round so as to avoid being spotted and got to Vikki's side unnoticed. He used his age old opening gambit with girls he knew but did not yet had carnal knowledge of.

"Of all the gin bars in all the world"

Ben was blissfully aware of the blatant misquote and had often joked with Stu that if he ever found a girl who corrected him he'd settle down and get married for she was clearly "the one". However, it looked like he was to wait a bit longer

"Ben!!!" Vikki said probably too enthusiastically due to the vodka "I didn't think you'd noticed or recognised me"

"Look at you Vikki, it's pretty difficult not to notice you! Need that glass topping up?"

They spent the next hour or so chatting and drinking and in spite of Suzi's warnings to be careful with this one, Vikki was having a great time and for the first time in his life Ben was actually enjoying the company of a girl rather than going along with it as a means to an end. The inevitable then happened

"Doo dooloo doo doo doo California Strut"

Stu did a double take when he saw Ben on the dance floor faux ballroom dancing with the girl he'd quite clearly set his targets on. By now he'd usually left, had moved on to plan B or had returned to the table screaming "next time Gadget!" in his best Doctor Claw voice. But not tonight, tonight he was actually dancing and had a beaming smile on his face. The main lights scorched everybody's retinas as they came on revealing the truth behind who people had been speaking to as they readjusted their vision to cope with the change. Ben looked at Vikki, her strawberry blonde hair looked amazing, much prettier than he'd remembered her from school and her eyes sparkled. She smiled at him and he felt a sensation in his stomach he'd never felt before. He immediately put this down to hunger and asked her if she fancied sharing a pizza. They joined the exodus down the narrow staircase out into the vast plain of the Riverhead Serengeti turned right and were soon ordering pizza.

Vikki felt a bit upset that, in spite of his reputation, Ben hadn't tried to kiss her. Buoyed by the bravado of a stomach full of vodka and a pulsing in her vagina each time Ben smiled she took the impetus and grabbed Ben and literally shoved her tongue in his mouth. Ben responded with gentle kisses and the pulsating in her fanny grew stronger. She thought she had had her first orgasm in the back of Scott's car the other week but this felt different, better even, but surely she wasn't having an orgasm from just kissing. "Take me home Ben" she caught herself saying much to her own surprise the warmth and moistness in her nether regions getting the better of her.

Kissing passionately in the taxi as they made the short journey to Ben's Welholme Road flat they were soon pressed against Ben's door as he expertly unlocked it without losing lip contact. He pushed her in and onto the stairs, lifting her skirt and ripping her tights as he started to lick and suck her now well engorged clitoris. A warmth and urgency begin flowing through her vagina like she had never experienced until she felt a release and what felt like a sea of liquid escaped from her all over Ben's chin. She now appreciated that whatever Scott had given her it was not an orgasm.

Kissing on the bed, Vikki reached down to Ben's boxer shorts. "Fucking hell it's massive" she gasped, no longer able to control her inner monologue. Ben smiled at her as he pushed her onto her back and slowly penetrated her, sliding all the way in causing the warmth, urgency and release to come quickly, and again, and again, and......

As the taxi turned towards New Waltham, Vikki shielded her eyes from the morning winter's sun. Tired yet satisfied, heady from a mixture of last night's booze and the spliff Ben had expertly rolled this morning, and with a soreness in her sex she smiled and promised herself to start going out a bit more.

# Chapter 7

PC Lucas Hughes inwardly sighed as he realised that he had been paired up with Sgt Davies again for tonight's shifts of driving round the streets of Grimsby and Cleethorpes apparently ignoring any crime that Davies deemed "petty" and in the way of him running his errands. Davies was an overweight man with a moustache that made Lucas feel that his fashion sense, along with his ambitions, had been left in the previous decade. Lucas despised Davies, particularly his insistance of people calling him "Dave" even though his real name was Stewart. Lucas hated nicknames as he thought it showed a lack of intelligence and was particularly keen on correcting anyone who tried to call him "Luke". Davies had picked this up and called him it pretty much constantly, even when it was not appropriate to even use a name. Davies was also fond of overusing "Hughesy" to get an extra rile out of Lucas.

Lucas had moved to Grimsby four months ago from his native Sheffield to join the Humberside force as he felt his aspirations to move up the chain quickly may have got lost in the larger South Yorkshire area. In that time Lucas had suffered what could only be described as institutionalised bullying, mainly centred on his Yorkshire roots with several inappropriate references to Peter Sutcliffe. The subject of ridicule also revolved around the time when, on one of his first shifts as a policeman, he had been knocked unconscious by a single punch by one of Grimsby Town's football hooligans apparently whom evaded his colleague's grasp as they were laughing at the incident. No justice had ever been brought against the perpatrator and the other policeman, especially Davies, seemed reluctant to give him any names as to who it may have been. He often promised himself he would do his utmost to make sure he imprisoned as many of the known hooligans as possible, however this seemed very difficult, especially when Davies pulled rank.

Lucas sat in the driver's seat of the patrol car and as always awaited Davie's instructions as to which way to go. He was too meek to speak out, but he really did resent being a state sponsored taxi driver to Davies's extracurricular activities.

"I think we'll go right tonight Hughesy" Davies spoke.

Lucas' hands clenched on the steering wheel, making his knuckles whiten, as he knocked on the indicator and headed down Victoria Street in the direction of the Docks. Following Davies' instructions they went over the Telegraph building flyover. As they approached Riby Square crossroads, a silver Vauxhall Nova pulled out in front of them, clearly jumping their red light and narrowly avoiding the front of the police car. Lucas slammed on the breaks, hit the lights and sirens and turned sharply right down Freeman Street in pursuit. The car pulled over and Lucas and Davies walked up to the driver's side window. The smell of alcohol permeated out as the driver wound it down.

"Yesh officer whatsh sheems to be the problem" slurred the driver at Lucas before his attention turned to his colleague.

Hey Copper Dave!! Look lads it's Copper Dave!! You alright pal?"

Davies nodded in recognition and suggested to Lucas that he go back to the car to perform the PNC check whilst he breathalysed the driver and then they could take him down to the nick. Lucas begrudgingly went back to the vehicle to radio it in and looked up. Davies had positioned himself so that he was looking directly at his back. The rain on the windscreen made it difficult to see but he could have sworn he saw him blowing into the pipe, not that he could say it under oath in a court of law.

"Well what d'you know?" said Davies returning to the car "absolutely sober as a judge!"

Lucas protested they should at least do him for dangerous driving and get him on the machine back at the station but Davies dismissed this quite offishly.

"Right then Lukey" Davies mocked "back down Cleethorpes Road"

It was obvious to Lucas where Davies was heading. A seedy little massage parlour on the main trunk road through to Cleethorpes called Nicole's. A drab, almost derelict, looking building which the owners had covered in bright pink vinyls on the windows with poorly drawn silhouettes of oddly proportioned women in allegedly sultry positions advertising to those who were clearly too stupid to understand the type of business on offer.

Much to the amusement of pretty much the whole town, the front of the premises invited potential customers to car parking facilities by proclaiming they should "use the rear entrance". Davies was one of many policeman in the town to utilise the subsidised rates given as a sweetener for turning a blind eye.

Lucas swang the car into the car park and Davies got out exclaiming that Lucas really should sample the wares himself. Lucas politely declined and smiled when Davies called him a puffter. Twenty minutes later a beaming, but slightly sweaty, Davies returned.

"Fucking love those foreign birds me. You ever had a foreign bird?"

"No"

"Fucking hell no need to go bright red"

It was true the conversation had made Lucas flush, but more out of anger than embarrassment.

"You ever even had a bird? You're either a virgin or a willy wuffter. Which is it?"

Lucas wanted to either plant a headbutt on Davies nose or tell him that yes he loved sucking cock but decided that either way would probably end up with a punch and he was subject to enough bullying at work without openly coming out, especially not to Davies. He gripped the wheel until his knuckles were nearly popping through the skin until the silence was broken by a call to a domestic nearby on Wellington Street.

A quite clearly heroin addled couple had let their argument spill over onto the street by which point a neighbour had dialled 999. Lucas and Davies arrived to find him straddled her on the path slapping both her cheeks with open palms. Lucas read the guy his rights whilst Davies took the drug ravaged girl inside. He came out five minutes later the girl crying and begging for him not to take it all.

The lanky desk sergeant Johnson smiled at Davies as they booked in the skinny bag head who'd been arrested.

"Any drugs found on the property?"

"Just these two bags and a few syringes" winked Davies at Johnson.

# Chapter 8

The pressure in Tim's chest built up once more, his limbs heavy, his heart pounding, the vice on his throat as his vocal cords dried up and he gasped for air, and the pressure on his chest, so much pressure....

He woke with a start, no Macca, not tonight. He pinched himself, his hands still shaking, his heart pounding, and a cold sweat over his body. He wasn't sure. Where was he hiding? Did he know about him and Hannah? Fuck man.

BANG BANG BANG

A loud angry knock at the door.

Jesus, its Macca. He's gonna burst the door open.

"TIM!"

A girl's voice

Groggy eyed Tim opens the door and Siobhan, a stuck up posh girl staying in his halls who he'd pissed off within days of starting is stood there angry faced.

"Phone for you - kindly tell your friends not to ring at this time of night some of us care about our studies"
"Oh ok sorry"

Tim looks at the clock. 4:23, who the fuck is ringing at this time on a Tuesday night? With a semi hard-on Tim clambers down the stairs to the reception hall of his hall of residence block where the communal phone is situated.

"Err......hello?"
"Timothy White. How the devil are you old chap?"

Ben's voice is comforting, this is the first time they've spoken since Tim moved away.

The "Well actually I think I'm going mental and keep predicting my own death at the hands of Macca because I fucked Hannah this summer" Tim wanted to say was replaced by "I'm good my friend. Why the fuck you ringing at half four on a Tuesday night?"

"You know. Tuesday night is student night at Gullies. Same time same place mate same time same place"

"Oh right so you're pissed?"

"Leathered mate and had a nice little smokey dokey"

"Cool so how's tricks"

"You know how it is, I'm still playing my music, still dreaming but it's stale in G.Y. mate absolutely stale, need a change of scene"

"Well aren't you still gigging all over?"

"Yeah mate but I mean day-to-day. Need to be somewhere where people will notice and stuff"

"So what you reckon mate?"

"Save up, maybe get a real 9 to 5, God forbid, wake up one morning and do one into the great yonder far from the great G.Y."

"Oh right mate, just as long as you send your address and number so your mates know you're alive"

"Of course my friend, of course, fucking hell mate this gear is strong"

"Lucky bastard I'm struggling out here, bit of squidgy black if I'm lucky and some grass"

"Mate this is from Thailand, proper fucking strong, highly giggly shit"

"Wiggy?"

Wiggy was a local dealer who somehow managed to get better grass than the rest. Rumours were most of it came from up his arse back from Amsterdam on the Hull ferry.

"Nah mate, some new contact I got, Copper Dave"

"For fuck sake man Copper Dave? He's a twat you know, just be careful"

"I will my good friend Timothy White I will"

"Just make sure you do mate, he's not to be trusted"

This was the real reason Tim hadn't introduced many people to Dave, he just didn't trust the fat moustached bastard as far as he could throw him, but more worryingly he wasn't that sure he could trust his friends much more. They carried on chewing the fat about this, that and the other. Tim was surprised at how much seemed to happen in Grimsby in 4 weeks compared to when you're actually there. He then popped the million dollar question.

"So how's the love life, met anyone special?"
"Yeah mate"

Tim nearly fell down in shock

"Only fucking kidding mate, tell me I nearly had you though?"
"Yeah nearly you sod"
"There was one girl though"

Ben stopped short of saying her name.

"Ginger girl, squirted all over my face, thought I was going to have to buy a new mattress, worth a double dip that one, felt, I don't know, different"

Tim listened to Ben rabbit on about his latest conquests chuckling.

"....trouble is though pal there's no sport in it anymore and I crave something different. I need some better excitement something other than hot dirty sex"

"You need to settle down"

"Wash your mouth out! But nah I just need something to help me escape, you know?"

"I know"

Tim looked up and out the window and was surprised to see the sun coming up. He sniffed his armpits and he reeked.

"Look mate I need a shower and I've got lectures in a bit"

"Ok sexy, make sure you get home soon."

"You sounds like my mam"

"Mmmm the sexy Lynn, you know I would don't you?"

"Fuck off!"

Tim put the receiver down and turned to head back upstairs when it rang again.

"Have you got a Super Nintendo?"
"Fuck off you daft bastard"

He hung up, turned and the same scenario happened.

"What?"
"Ah Timothy, of all the gin bars in all the world"
"Its joints you daft cunt"
"It sure is!"

Tim heard the flint of the lighter and a big deep breath before Ben exhaled giggling.

"Love you and miss you dude"

In the shower Tim grabbed the shower gel and gave it a sniff, he wasn't overly enamoured and resolved that maybe he should actually buy his own. He let the water run over his body before giving his armpits and his perineum a good scrub before stepping out and realising he'd forgotten his towel. Fuck it he thought to himself as he grabbed his clothes and walked back to his room making no effort to shield any passers by a full eyeful of his manhood. He got to his room and started to think about Hannah. He felt guilty for not ringing or writing to her to let her know his contact details and he missed her but he knew it could never work until she was at least 18 and preferably without any interference from her psychopath of a brother. He got changed, grabbed his bag and headed off to lectures.

# Chapter 9

Bobby White sat in his usual place in the Jubilee public house and finished his pint of beer. He sat staring at the glass and watched the white foam run down to the bottom. The answer wasn't in the bottom of this one either, it never fucking was. He got up to go to the bar to get himself another. It was poured before he even got there. Bobby caught a glimpse of himself in the mirror, he didn't like what he saw - he was only 42 yet he looked well in excess of his age, the greying around his temples accentuating his deathly pallor and the puffiness around his eyes and jowls making him look severely overweight.

He thought back to when he was a young man and he first met his Lynn. He had been quite a handsome guy and was earning good money at the refinery. Lynn had got pregnant within 3 months of them first dating so it was a shotgun style trip to the registry office with everyone saying it wouldn't last. The exuberance of youth and early throws of lust and love telling them otherwise. They (the other people) were right, of course, but he did have the happiest days of his life with Lynn. If you'd asked Lynn she would give a different definition of the happiest days of your life and that did not involve staying at home with the children Tim and Karl and waiting for Bobby to get home from the pub and awaiting the fist or belt or whatever was coming that night. They'd split up not long after Bobby's accident at work which had made him spend even more time in the pub consoling his sorrows and greatly diminishing his compensation payout. She'd got with Ray, a colleague from the hotel, soon after and never looked back.

Returning to his seat Bobby looked at his watch, 12:10. He took a sip of his pint, wiped the froth of his top lip and started studying the form. He'd finish this pint then take the half mile walk onto the Willows to the bookies. He liked the Wybers but one thing it was missing was a bookies. It was ok though, he could always pop in the Valiant for a livener before heading back, besides he preferred Mike in the Valiant to Steve in the Jube anyway and wished they could swap landlords. Bobby circled his horses for the day's meetings as Paul and John walked in.

"Eh up, where's George and Ringo?"

Bobby joked in the time old manner that Paul and John accepted from their fellow pisshead that they both assumed was much older than them. In reality they had at least ten years on him, the drink destroying his visage and figure much quicker than their own. Bobby finished his pint, watching the foam descend in his usual way then grabbed his coat, turned up his collar and went out into the drizzle to go lay his probably unsuccessful bets.

The quick livener in the Valiant turned into three pints, all with whisky chasers, as Bobby celebrated his first two horses coming in on a double. Watching the remaining bubbles of the third Bobby grabbed his coat, turned up his collar once again and braved the walk back to his seat in the Jube. By now his legs were feeling the effects of the booze but at least his hands had stopped shaking. The cold rain on his face had a slightly sobering effect but the recent whisky gave his stomach a warm glow. As he crossed over back onto Wybers Way, he noticed a familiar face smiling and holding hands with a pretty young girl.

ΔΔΔ

With just a couple of tokes of Martin's spliff in him Karl had started to feel the relaxation from a shitty day at school when he boarded the 45 to get home. He sat next to Gemma and spoke to her and Hannah. Not that he could be certain but he could have sworn Gemma's hand was brushing his - choosing to ignore it just in case he'd got the wrong signals and to save himself embarrassment. As the bus pulled into Great Coates, Karl felt a definite squeeze of his hand as his and Gemma's fingers interlocked and he felt his cock begin to stiffen when her thumb delicately stroked against his palm. Adjusting his position to hide his growing erection Karl began to feel uncomfortable. Gemma must have noticed his trousers begin to grow as she leant forward and whispered in his ear.

"I can't wait to taste that,"

This made Karl even harder and he could feel the pre-cum start to dribble out of his Jap's eye. He adjusted position once more in a futile attempt to hide his hard penis and was desperate to make sure Hannah hadn't noticed Gemma's advances on him. Uncomfortably Karl stood up, rang the stop bell and walked down the stairs of the bus. Alighting at the layby at the bottom of Wybers Way. They crossed over and walked across the grass verge to Mayfair Drive, Gemma making excuses about borrowing a CD from Karl so that she could come onto the Wybers rather than home to the Willows estate. They said their goodbyes to Hannah and when she was out of sight Gemma once again held Karl's hand and preceded in telling him explicitly all the things she was going to do to his now fully engorged cock.

"TIM!!, TIM!!"

Karl turned round as, despite their different coloured hair, this wasn't the first time he'd been mistaken for his elder brother. It was, however, the first time the mistake had been made by a family member. His heart sank at the thought of having to speak to his Dad who would, by this time in the afternoon, almost certainly be pissed. He knew that the chances of ejaculating by means of Gemma would diminish greatly with every passing second of talking to this old alky.

"It's Karl, Dad,"
"Of course it is! Karl my son!"

Bobby extended his hand for a handshake which Karl felt was strange and uncomfortable. Reciprocating, Karl found a rolled up bit of paper in his Dad's hand, looking down he saw a purple hue of a twenty pound note and his feelings of resentment to his father lifted slightly. In all his formative years this was the only time he could remember his Dad giving him money.

"Just has a nice win on the nags, treat yourself and your girlfriend. What's your name darl?"

Gemma introduced herself but neither she nor Karl corrected Bobby's assumption on their relationship status.

"How's my lovely wife?"

"Mum's fine, so is Ray" Karl replied making it obvious to Bobby that Lynn was no longer any of his business and in a tone to beg him not to come round causing trouble again.

"I didn't ask about that Jew faced bastard" - Karl hated his Dad using such inappropriate and dated insults. He rolled his eyes at Gemma as if to say sorry.

"Dad, please,"

"Alright son, for you, but only for you. Anyway see up there son?"

He pointed towards the pebble dashed exterior of the Jubilee Inn

"Mecca is calling and as you well know I always like to give Steve some of my winnings,"

"OK dad we'll walk up with you,"

Leaving Bobby at his second home they carried on walking towards Karl's house, stopping briefly for a long impassioned kiss that made Karl's cock spring to life again. Pushing the door open another passionate kiss in the hallway as Gemma's hand found Karl's zip and unleashed his cock stroking it slowly. A globule of pre-cum dripped onto the hallway carpet and he scuffed it semi-clean with his foot. Gemma got to her knees and circled his wet bell end with her hungry tongue. Karl grabbed a handful of Gemma's curly brown hair as he pushed her head further onto his cock forcing her to gag. Releasing the grip a little he let her slide up and down his shaft with her eager mouth, her tongue flicking Karl's bell end and frenulum. His bell end started to tingle and Karl felt the warmth at the base of his cock as his balls began to tighten as he pumped hot semen into Gemma's mouth. Gemma looked up at Karl, showed him a mouthful of cum then swallowed it before cleaning his spent dick with her mouth.

"Now," she said "Get your arse upstairs, it's my turn,"

Karl had slept with plenty of girls, he had just never felt the desire, or had been asked, to give them oral pleasure so this was a first for him and with Gemma's reputation he didn't want to be shit. He remembered watching porn with Martin once where the annoying American woman on it was giving a tutorial on oral sex so he tried to remember everything she said. Sucking on Gemma's labia and tonguing the opening to her hole he savoured the muskiness and was surprised at the faint sweetness. He suddenly remembered the woman's advice about exposing the clitoris so he carefully, and in his own mind expertly, pushed up on Gemma's pubis and started sucking the area. Gemma's moans indicated to him that he had certainly remembered correctly and most importantly he had found the right area.

"Mmm yes,"

"MMMMMM,"

"AAAAAARGH! WHAT THE ACTUAL FUCK?!"

∆ ∆ ∆

Ben had woken up with a stinking hangover. It was mid-afternoon already, and he'd wasted another day which he probably should have been spending writing new music or sending his demos to record companies. He decided that as seen as the best part of the day had gone he may as well waste the rest of it.

He thought back to last night's conversation with Tim and how he'd nearly admitted that he was becoming obsessed with Vikki. Oh Vikki, with her gorgeous strawberry blonde hair, pretty eyes and that arse he just couldn't get out of his thoughts no matter how hard he had tried. His feelings for her were certainly different to anything he'd experienced with any other girls, for a start he could remember her name almost three weeks after. He laid back and thought about her, putting his hands in his boxer shorts and slowly teasing his foreskin and squeezing his bell end. He was soon hard and frantically stroking away his hangover with his right hand while squeezing his balls with his left. In no time at all his stomach was covered in his warm juice. He got up, had a shower, dried off and got changed then left the house to borrow the CDs and videos he and Tim had spoken about.

Arriving at Tim's house he knocked as loud as he could three times then went round the back. It looked like nobody was home. Ben knew where they hid the spare key so let himself in, poured himself a juice before making his way upstairs to Tim's room. He heard the familiar sounds of a girl enjoying herself coming from young Karl's room so decided to take a peek at what was going on. Karl's bare arse was in the air as a girl lay on her back, legs spread while Karl was eating her pussy. Ben assessed the girl - pretty, brunette curls, reasonable boobs but probably a little on the young side for him. He stood and watched for a minute until the girl opened her eyes and made direct eye contact with him.

"AAAAAARGH! WHAT THE ACTUAL FUCK?!"

Karl stopped what he was doing, looked at Gemma and followed her eye line to an inanely grinning Ben who started laughing.

"Get in there young Karl White,"

"Ben,"

Karl didn't know whether to be angry or laugh. Gemma, initially put off by the intruder was now a bit more relaxed as she realised who the stranger was and his reputation which went before him. Ben and Gemma had never met although had heard of each other. Gemma more interested in Ben than the other way around.

"Are you just gonna fucking stand there, or you gonna come and join us?"

"Karl?"

"I'm game if you are,"

Ben pondered for a moment then kicked off his trainers and pulled off his T-shirt and jeans and hopped into Karl's now considerably cosy single bed. Gemma the middle of the sandwich started playing with both boy's cocks until Ben moved down and started sucking her left breast. He motioned for Karl to take the other and he duly obliged. Fingers everywhere on Gemma's pussy and both nipples being sucked a very loud orgasm built up inside her. Karl and

Gemma becoming very compliant to Ben's puppet mastery as he directed his own porn movie in his head. He eventually settled on getting Gemma to position herself on all fours as he slid underneath her and into her pussy while making sure Karl was ready to penetrate her anus.

# Chapter 10

Katie was annoyed, really fucking pissed off. With herself more than anything. What a mug! And him! That bastard! Mark, what an absolute twat.

She knew there would be trouble when she said she was fine with him still being friends with his ex, Jess, and she doubted herself when the words came out of her mouth. Her friends all warned her too and now they would be proven right and she knew Dani, who was most vocally against it, would be so fucking smug.

Katie thought it was odd that Mark had insisted on going out in Cleethorpes tonight but had gone along with it. The reason was obvious when they were in the pub and Jess walked in dolled up to the nines. Her heels clicked on the floor as she made her way over to where Mark and Katie were sat. Her 12 denier hold ups barely hidden by the dress she was wearing. "That fucking bitch" thought Katie knowing that Jess knew exactly what that attire would do to Mark's loins.

She had been apprehensive at first when Mark had described his foot and stocking fetish but had gone along with it out of her wants to keep a guy she liked. It turned out she actually quite liked the attention he gave her feet and particularly liked the feeling of his hot semen seeping through the nylon of her stockings after giving him a foot job. There was no way she was going to give him up, especially not to Jess, absolutely no way.

Katie saw the look on Mark's face as he surveyed Jess's contours in the dress and his eyes stayed on the heels far too long for her liking. She had to admit Jess looked sexy and this just made her paranoia about the situation much worse. But was she really being paranoid? She'd always suffered with panic attacks and her counsellors had taught her methods to question her anxieties but none of these were working right now. She realised Mark was up to something and she didn't like it one bit.

Katie had gone to the bar and reluctantly included Jess in the round. Pint for Mark and a double vodka and coke for her and Jess. For good measures she ordered an extra vodka and necked it at the bar while waiting for her change. As she returned to the table she could have sworn she'd seen Mark's hand on Jess' thigh squeezing what would be the outline of the lacy hold up top band. She chalked this off to her anxiety and made excuses to go to the toilet. She didn't need the toilet she just needed to escape and breathe out the panic attack that was brewing. Plus she needed a fag and Mark thought she'd given up.

Coming back down the stairs she paused as she saw Jess stroking the hair on the back of Mark's neck. Who the fuck did she think she was? And him? He'd fucking arranged all this too. She saw crimson. She wanted to slap the taste out of both their mouths. Storming up to the table she threw her bag at Jess and her drink, well glass, at Mark and stormed out into the night's heavy rain, nearly knocking the unsuspecting bouncer over in the process.

So here she was, tottering down Isaac's Hill in her heels with tears smudging her mascara down her face and her hair plastered down from the pouring rain. She had no money for a taxi as her bag and it's contents were scattered all over the pub floor. Cold, dejected and desperate she had started to walk home.

"Fuck it!"

Her night was summed up as her heel caught in an excessively large gap in the pavement causing it to snap. No amount of grovelling was going to get that bastard back in her good books even if he brought her best handbag back.

Her skin hurt from the cold and rain. What she would give for her coat or the warmth of the pub where those two fuckers were probably kissing and canoodling right now laughing at her. Her bare feet ached as they pounded the cold pavement of Brereton Avenue. Tears still running down her face and a knot in her stomach as a panic attack built inside her, threatening to take her under. She entered Sidney Park, sat on a swing and sobbed.

Reaching for her non-existent bag for a cigarette she cursed Mark and Jess. "Pair of fucking bas...." a hand grabbed her from behind and pulled her towards the bushes. She tried to scream but it was muffled by a hand and adrenaline had paralysed her vocal cords. Her heart pounded in her chest as she saw the swings disappearing, kicking her legs as hard as her fear ridden body would allow but the grip on her was too tight. She bit down on the gloved hand and heard a man gasp, release the grip slightly then hit the bridge of her nose with a clenched fist. She saw stars as the pain emanated from her nose and she tasted the metallic taste of blood. She felt the sharpness of the branches from the bushes as her assailant's hands lifted her dress and the other gloved hand forcefully penetrated her vagina, ripping the labia on the way.

Time distorted, seconds became hours as she was subject to excruciating pain as a sheathed penis entered her from behind ripping her perianal skin akin to an episiotomy. He thrusted violently over and over until she felt his knees weaken and his cock twitch his orgasm. The grip was released and she fell to the floor.

Through the tears she saw a man wearing a black balaclava running away toward Queen Mary's Avenue.

Δ Δ Δ

Neil was a Grimsby lad through and through so when he'd finished his journalism degree and he saw the position advertised at the Grimsby Evening Telegraph he jumped at the opportunity. What a mistake that had turned out to be. He'd been here 18 months and the most exciting job he had was covering the local dance festival. He daydreamed of a big scoop. His senior colleague Tony threw something on his desk without reading it.

"Fancy a piece on bike locks?"

The press release from Humberside Police skidded to a halt and Neil picked it up. Reading it once, taking a breath and reading it again slowly his eyes widened as he pieced together the jigsaw that the police seemed to have missed. "Surely not" he thought to himself as images of the stories he'd evaluated for his A-level came into his head.

He spent the next hour in the archives with the help of Sabrina the intern and then felt confident enough to write his story typing faster than he thought possible. He then took the deepest of inhales as, hands trembling, he picked up the receiver and dialled the editor.

That evening the Grimsby Evening Telegraph ran Neil's story on the front page with the headline

"IS THE BEAST BACK?"

∆ ∆ ∆

The doors to the investigation room burst open with exceptional force as Morris (who was meant to be on annual leave) exploded through them grasping a crumpled copy of the Evening Telegraph in his left fist. The vermillion shade on his face indicated that the volume knob was about to get turned up and some severe shouting and expletives were going to be heard. Somebody was in for a bollocking of monumental proportions. He raised his hand and pointed at the closest DI - "YOU!" - his pointed finger alternating between the detective's throat and the headline on the paper.

"Bu.....Bu......But you're on holiday Sir"

Morris erupted into a four letter tirade - "Something as significant as this and none of you fuckers think to involve me? I bet not a single one of you put two and two fucking together did you? Fucking no! I have to fucking learn about this off some spotty journalist cunt at the Tellywag who's got more fucking brains to piece this together than any of you dumb twats"

The Evening Telegraph spread out like confetti as it was launched across the room at the first poor soul brave enough to attempt an apology - "I don't care if I'm in a fucking coma - another case like this you involve me!"

# 1999

# Chapter 11

"It's been dry for months" Dave said to his associate Ron as he bemoaned that he hadn't been involved in the fruits of a fortuitous drugs bust for a long time with much lament - "It's really buggering up my pension plan and stocks are nearly out".

Dave had always supplemented his earnings with a little bit of sidelined mischief but recently he had been earning so much on the side that it was almost like he was supplementing his mischief by being a policeman. What started out as a bribe here and there, usually from mates (or mates of mates), had turned into what some people with a different moral compass would probably call corruption. Dave's main source of income was cannabis. Dividing what someone was possessing into what they were being arrested for (approximately 25%) and his own stash (the rest). Charging his select customer base slightly under market value so that everyone was a winner - except the poor sods who'd been arrested obviously. Although the way the idiots at the Grimsby tellywag reported street value, you'd think Dave could have retired long ago - he did not understand where they got their prices from and had often wondered about seeing who he needed to supply there as they were clearly being ripped off. Now though, he was down to his last few ounces of weed and his lock up needed replenishing urgently. He did however seem to have an inexplicably over supply of heroin, also acquired through ill-gotten means.

"What we need to do" said Ron "is turn a few of these stoners into smackheads then we'd be quids in, laughing all the way to the bank."

Ron was a recently retired copper of similar virtues and had taken Dave under his wing when he started at the nick. Dave went through his client list in his head and very quickly came up with a perfect one. He'd been waiting for an excuse to get at this one since he fucked his niece Charlotte and now he had the perfect opportunity.

It was only a matter of days before Dave got a chance to perform his master plan. Normally he'd be annoyed if a text came halfway through his game of Snake but this one brought a large, deliriously happy smile to his face.

HI DAVE. FANCY A MCDONALDS? I'LL BUY U A QUARTER POUNDER

It wasn't exactly the Enigma code but Dave was happy that he'd get away with it with the right colleague. Plus anyway he'd be meeting him at McDonalds so the story kind of married up. He smiled as he thought how to carefully word his reply. It was going to give him such gratification to take this bastard down such a nasty pathway.

JUST A BURGER. I'M ON A DIET IM STARTING 2 LOOK LIKE HENRY 8 MEET U @ 7?

He was quite smug with himself, contently he returned to moving the increasingly growing rectangle across the screen in search of the pixelated dots. This time he was pissed off as a text interrupted him.

LET ME GET BACK 2 U

* * * * *

Ben left the message with the operator for Wiggy's pager and immersed himself back to the Nintendo 64 and Goldeneye. He laughed as he recalled the stoned joke that he and Stu had had at Wiggy's expense the other week. Wiggy didn't have a mobile as he "didn't trust them and they'll never catch on" whereas Stu's theory was he just wanted to keep his pager because it made him feel like Ice Cube in "Fuck Tha Police" and that Wiggy was short for wigger. Ben reasoned that the real reason probably lay somewhere between the two. He waited for the return call from the pager message. Half an hour later the phone eventually rang.

"Hello."
"Alright pal?"
"Alright Wiggy? How's it going?"
"Dry pal, dry."

"Fuck!"

"Sorry pal."

"Not even any Sputnik?"

"No mate not enough to be sharing."

"Fuck!"

"Sorry blue I really am."

"Ok mate see you around."

Ben put the receiver down and cursed loudly. With an air of discontent he picked up his Nokia to text Dave back to tell him he'd take the eighth of an ounce when suddenly he remembered another outlet. Looking through the phone book he found the only number for a Riley in Laceby and rang.

"Hello?"

"Oh hi. Is erm.....erm...... Riles there?"

"We're all called Riles mate. Which one you after?"

Ben hung up saying nothing realising he didn't know much about Riles other than he was one of Karl's mates who dealt a bit of weed every now and then. Not giving up he texted Tim.

WHATS UR KARLS M8 RILES NAME?

Within a minute he got a reply.

FUCKED IF I KNOW. HIS NAMES RILES!

WHATS UR KARLS NO?

After bouncing a load of three way texts it was established that Riles was also out of gear but would bear Ben in mind next time he was in supply because Karl had vouched for him. Reluctantly and with a heavy heart Ben messaged Dave.

OI HENRY U STILL WANT THAT BURGER?

∆ ∆ ∆

Dave hadn't stopped smiling since the text had come through and planned as meticulously as he could how he would play this. He decided that putting a few wraps of brown in the bag and not saying anything was the best way. "This dumb bastard won't be able to help himself" he thought as he positioned the wraps so they weren't obvious then set off into town towards McDonalds.

Ben sat in the usual place. Money already inside the burger box compliant and well versed in deals with Dave. Dave sat down opposite him placed his burger box side by side with Ben's. They chatted quickly about Town's indifferent start to the season whilst eating their fries, Dave smothering them in ketchup much to Ben's visible disgust. They agreed that Lester and Ashcroft was the preferable strike partnership before Dave arose picking up the burger box and thus completing the deal. Ben decided not to tell Dave that his tache was covered in ketchup. "Scruffy fat bastard" he thought.

Before heading home Ben decided that he'd probably earned himself at least a pint. He popped into the Sheaf to refresh himself and whilst savouring the lager's bubbles and hoppy freshness on his tongue he pondered that the 3 days he had gone without sex was far too long. The brunette who was sat as an obvious third wheel with her friend and her date, was (all things considered) reasonably cute and her posture, along with the glint in her eye, told Ben she was an obvious slag. Making eyes at her he saw his opportunity as she went to the bar. He pounced. It was all too easy as she succumbed to his charms and they were back at his Welholme Road flat within the hour.

A few hours later as the girl whose name he'd already forgotten's taxi pulled away, Ben sat at his desk with a familiar and satisfying ache in his balls. He rolled the tobacco out of a cigarette into the expertly crafted L-shaped Rizla papers before him. Taking the bag out of his coat pocket he opened it and inhaled a nostril full of its sweet, almost sweaty, aroma. He put his fingers in the bag and felt the folded paper, pulling it out and unwrapping it. He inspected the sand like substance inside. Dave must have been having an off day he thought to himself as he wrapped the powder back up and threw the papers into his sock drawer. Thinking no more of it he finished crafting the joint, roaching it with some of the Rizla packet. He clicked the Freeserve button on the computer to connect to the internet. The bings and bongs of the modem connecting via his phone line like an old Commodore loading a game felt reassuring as he leant back, lit and inhaled his well-earned smoke. He contemplated and thought “I really must get out of this town”.

# Chapter 12

Despite being them themselves, Ian and Tim didn't really care that much for students so a Friday night down at the Union's venue "The Basement" for the "Friday Night Disco" probably seemed like an odd choice of night out. It was, however, Freshers Week which meant, as Ian had pointed out frequently, there would be plenty of "fanny" who didn't know what a pair of dicks they were yet.

Starting early they were mixing pints of half brandy and half Coke. The brandy procured from Netto for the princely sum of £5.50 a litre was every bit as vile as its price would suggest - more suited for thinning paint or cleaning gloss brushes. At about 7:30 the brandy had all gone so Tim took the short trip over the road to the shop to get some beers, more fags and some green Rizlas. As he got back Ian had the Charlatans

CD case on his lap and was chopping out two very large lines.

"Straighten us up a bit before we head out" he proclaimed as Tim opened a can each and rolled up a £10 note. The familiar taste in the back of his throat as the numbness in his nose hit. Buzzing off the cheap brandy and cocaine they left their rented Ashgrove house and made their way up a street to see what delights were to be had in Delius bar this evening.

So called as it was situated in a building next door to where the composer Frederick Delius apparently lived, Delius bar was a brightly lit, very spacy pub that was frequented by students and locals alike. Tim had been initially drawn to Delius as it was branded an "It's A Scream" bar by the brewery and therefore was almost exactly the same as the Wheatsheaf back in Grimsby.

Tim went to the bar as Ian took a turn left towards the toilet to powder his nose. Over to his right were a group of girls in their red netball team jumpers playing drinking games with other girls who were clearly freshers trying to get initiated onto the team. This was one of the things he hated about students and in particular the sports teams with their stupid jumpers and drinking games. He knew that there'd be a few of those cunts at the FND tonight. He looked over at the netball girls and vaguely recognised a peroxide blonde chubby looking girl with a low cut top on that was showing an immense amount of cleavage. He got his round and headed in the opposite direction toward the pool table and Ian who was chatting to a couple of local lads that they had bought Charlie from in the past.

Leaving Delius and walking past the imposing Richmond building, Tim felt Ian almost holding his hand as he dropped the tablet in it.

"Thought a Mitzy might help the evening along."

Inspecting the vaguely pink tablet, Tim noticed the Mitsubishi logo stamped on the side. He put it in his mouth and nearly gagged trying to swallow it with no liquid.

"God that tasted rank."

"I know but it'll be worth it."

Ian's face lit up in a familiar look of mischief and buggerment that Ben knew all too well as he seemingly forgot about the young impressionable freshers he'd been mentioning all week.

Walking past their old Kirkstone Halls, Tim was reminded of the panic attack inducing nightmares he used to have in there and how they stopped when they moved out. They saw Jon attired in his black jumper. The black jumper showed to the rest of the students that he was in the football team but to Ian and Tim indicated he was a bit of a cunt.

"Wahey I've had a couple of cans and missed the social. I'm gonna get fined but fuck it. You Zulu warrior."

Tim was under no illusions whatsoever now that Jon was indeed a cunt of the highest order.

Walking down to the basement they gave each other a wry smile as Jon departed to the rest of the black jumpered wankers and they made their way to the bar to consume bottles of sickly sweet alcopops whilst they waited for their tablets to dissolve and course their way into their brains. The alcopop of choice, Reef, was always on offer in union bars at £1.25 a bottle or 4 bottles for a fiver and Ian and Tim always took the piss out of people struggling to carry 4 bottles and drink at the same time. If you pointed out to anyone that the offer wasn't actually an offer they would look sheepishly at you as it dawned on them and make excuses about not having to queue. This never resonated with Tim as he'd been to Millwall away so pushing in front of Tarquin the Peace Studies student from the Home Counties didn't exactly fill him with fear.

They stood watching people assessing the situation as Tim felt butterflies rising from his stomach. Ian looked at him grinning, his pupils getting visibly bigger and offered him some gum. Tim kept noticing the peroxide blonde with the cleavage but still couldn't place where he knew her from. She'd looked at him a couple of times too with a similar look of confusion.

As the endorphins trickled into his brain, a profuse and formidable wave of love encircled Tim and he needed to hug someone. Dancing on the spot with moves incongruous to the cheesy pop music being blared out of the sound system, Tim looked over to Ian who by now was completely out of control of his bottom lip. The bass and the tinny kick drums taking over his arms and legs as he smiled. Ian winked at Tim as he walked away and over to a group of girls. One of the girls was Rosie who Ian had slept with a few times. Tim wasn't fond of her for several reasons. Firstly she'd turned him down in first year as she had overheard one of his most vivid Macca dreams and thought he was mentally unstable, secondly she ate fried egg and peanut butter sandwiches which was just plain weird and lastly, and probably most importantly in Tim's eyes Rosie was from Scunthorpe - meaning that Tim had an inherent hatred of her. Ian was holding court with Rosie and her group of girls so Tim decided to do a circuit of the basement to see if he could find anyone to talk bollocks to. It wasn't long when he found "Little Jim" (who had lived in halls in first year) trying his hardest to pin peroxide cleavage girl up against a wall. Jim looked a mess in his ill-fitting red rugby jumper; at least three sizes too small due to excess alcohol bulk and washing machine shrinkage. Peroxide cleavage girl was clearly unimpressed by his advances and seemed relieved to see Tim.

"Aren't you from Grimsby?"

"Yeah, Wybers. You too?"

"Yeah Keelby, you went to Healing didn't you? Karl White's brother?"

"Yeah that's me. Tim pleased to meet you."

"Nicola. By the way my face is up here!"

Tim was kind of embarrassed to have been caught blatantly staring at the mightily impressive breasts but Nicola had squeezed them together when mentioning her face so he figured that all wasn't that bad. Jim skulked off to try his caveman technique on another unsuspecting netball girl. They found seats and Tim went and bought drinks, this time reasoning that getting 4 would buy him more time to speak to Nicola.

"It's the same price per bottle if you buy one or four you know" she said as he sat back down, placing two bottles full of the gaudy orange drink in front of her.

The ecstasy in Tim's system made it easy for him to chat and he felt comfortable in Nicola's presence. They chatted for a good hour about home and mutual associates and it transpired that Nicola was staying in the exact same room as Tim in Kirkstone Halls, studying the same course. All the time Tim getting caught looking at her cleavage followed by Nicola squeezing her arms against her breasts to press them together and then reminding Tim where her eyes were.

"You coming back to your old room for a night cap?" Nicola bravely said as the main lights lit the vast expanse of the basement. Tim agreed and Nicola held his hand as they walked back, stopping briefly to kiss passionately, Tim finding great pleasure in running his hands through her peroxide locks.

"Forgive all the kelter everywhere I've not really unpacked yet," Nicola said as she undid the door before sitting on the bed and pouring two big measures of vodkas into mugs. Sipping the vodka Tim's mind was everywhere other than the particular job in hand.

"You've been looking at them all night Tim, come here and kiss me and I'll let you play with them."

The combination of booze and ecstasy made the skin contact feel exceptionally pleasurable as Tim's cock sprung half to life and he managed to maintain it enough to get in and bring Nicola to orgasm. There was no way, however, this was going to make him cum. Faking ejaculation Tim withdrew, removed the condom and proceeded to hug Nicola, slowly kneading her huge mammaries as he drifted off to sleep in the single bed.

The pressure developed in Tim's chest. So much pressure. His throat tightened. A tinnitus inducing wave of blood hit Tim's auditory system. Heart pounding like a sledgehammer he woke with a start covered in sweat Macca was sat at the desk smoking a cigarette and crying.

"I think I might be the beast."
"What you talking about Macca?"
"The rapist - I'm sure it is me."

Tim felt a rush of blood to his head which quickly drained to his cock as he felt the warm rush of ejaculation and a satisfying orgasm. The panic developed again - pressure, tightness, heartbeats, audible screams - really audible screams.

"What the fuck you doing?"

"Eh?"

"You sick bastard you've wanked onto my back - Get the fuck out my room."

# Chapter 13

"Good result that" Simon turned round and said to Ben. He was right a 1-1 draw with Birmingham was a good result.

"Aye," Ben agreed "Bradley Allen took his goal well."

"Sure did. See you next match?"

"Yeah mate, same time same place."

Ben walked down the steps of the Pontoon and left Blundell Park for what would be the last time. Skilfully avoiding getting dog shit on his Wallabies on Imperial Ave he nearly bumped into a group of excited looking teenagers in Burberry caps as he heard the chanting from the Birmingham mob in Harrington Street. He smiled to himself as the capped youths ran off remembering the mischief he, Tim and their friends used to get up to and was glad he was out of it.

Crossing the road and into McDonalds checking his phone to make sure his meeting with Dave was still going ahead. Once again Dave would only sell him a Louis the Sixteenth rather than the quarter he wanted, and he'd been inexplicably putting wraps of heroin in the bags for a few weeks now so much so he had probably enough in his sock drawer to get an elephant off their tits. Ben had put this down to getting two customer's orders mixed up but when Dave had asked if there was "anything else" he wanted at the last exchange he was beginning to have doubts, particularly after the warnings he'd had.

The burger box swap went ahead as planned and Ben made his way back to his flat to get sorted for tomorrow. Only stopping for one quick pint on the way home and not even surveying the ladies in the pub that intently. He got back to the now practically empty flat. Sitting down with a spliff he began to write his explanatory note to everybody. Re-reading it made him sob as he thought of his Mum's reaction to it and he wanted to say happier things. Ripping it up he grabbed another sheet of paper and began again. Once more the note made him sad, and he eventually settled on the fifth draft which was succinct yet explained it all perfectly.

Δ Δ Δ

For late October the weather was particularly mild and Lucas was having possibly his best day as a policeman since starting. He had never seen Davies so animated and enthusiastic, it was almost as if he was a genuine policeman today. He'd even written a ticket for someone who'd jumped a red light which was practically unheard of. He was being pleasant and for a change didn't smell of stale alcohol nor had he used any coarse, racist or homophobic language.

"It's a good Sabbath Lucas, I've got a good feeling about today" Dave exclaimed. And he did have a good feeling. He thought to himself that if that bastard wasn't going to be dumb enough to take any of the heroin then he would have had enough in his flat to send him down for a good length of time, particularly if he planted some more too. "Shall we take a trip down

Welholme Road?" Dave asked almost too cheerily. Lucas didn't question Dave's newly found attitude as he found it pleasing.

Driving from the Town centre leisurely Lucas even noticed Dave whistling a tune. He parked the car near People's Park as they then crossed over and down the drive of the house which had flats at the rear. "If you'd be so kind to let me deal with this Lucas" Dave said kindly "although I suspect this druggy will be stoned or hungover and still in bed". He knocked loudly on the door.

After the third unanswered knock Dave tried the handle to find it open. Slowly creeping up the stairs they found an empty yet tidy flat with a solitary note on the telephone table at the top of the stairs.

"Fucking Bastard!" Dave shouted as he read it.

Lucas prepared himself to see a hanging corpse as he searched the remaining rooms to no avail.

Dave just let the note drop to the floor.

Sorry Mum,

Have had enough of this town.

Have moved to London.

Will be in touch
Love Ben xx

"I am gonna get that bastard!" Dave said out loud but not within earshot of Lucas before placing a large dent in the kitchen cupboard with his fist.

∆ ∆ ∆

Liam Gallagher's voice slowed and became deeper as the batteries ran out on his Walkman. Ben stood on the platform of Doncaster train station three hours later than planned. He'd fallen asleep and woken up just as the train was pulling into Stockport so he had had to get the train back to Donny to catch a later Kings Cross train than he had planned. Boarding with all his worldly possessions - one bag of clothes and his guitar - he felt a pang of guilt for not telling his Mum and leaving the note at the top of the stairs for her to find as she went to pick him up for Sunday dinner.

He'd been planning his escape from the mundanity of Grimsby for weeks. Using the web to find a bedsit near London Bridge and a nearby menial but reasonably paid job. He'd surreptitiously started giving away things he deemed to be surplus to requirements and now he was actually doing it. He was leaving G.Y. and he was going to take his music seriously, very seriously. He'd already scouted out a live music venue near his new digs that was his destination for this evening where he would go and talk to people about the local scene and where he could find band mates and most importantly paid gigs. The planning of his getaway had given him a newly found zest, and he had written nearly an albums worth of new songs that he knew were better than half the rubbish being released nowadays. He knew the world was ready to hear his music - he just needed to focus. Calm down on the weed and the vagina and concentrate.

After taking the tube the wrong way he eventually got to the letting agents. There was an incompetent, yet fuckable, girl on the front desk and Ben had images of sleeping rough when at first she couldn't find his paperwork. The panic alleviated by an elder colleague. As he wandered around his new neighbourhood looking for his new flat, he got lost passing the same corner shop at least seven times before eventually going in to buy fags, Rizla papers and bravely asking directions. Today could only get better he thought as he eventually unlocked the door to his new abode.

His new home, if one could be as bold as to call it such, comprised a bed, a cooker and a washing machine in one room and a shower cum toilet room next door, all for four times the rent he'd been paying for his 2 bed flat in Grimsby. But hey, it was London, the Big Smoke, and after all, that was the sacrifice he was going to have to make as an artist.

He was starving, so he looked in his bag and all he had was a Kit-Kat. Cursing himself for not buying food at the shop he carefully removed the outer paper, then the foil, his mild form of OCD taking over as he folded them both neatly and laid them on the top of the bin. He ate it so quickly he may as well have inhaled it before he sat down and rolled a spliff. Taking a big inhale he felt himself begin to relax. Stubbing it out after only smoking half he went to have a shower before going out to the venue around the corner, hoping this time he wouldn't get lost.

He sat on his own, drinking, listening to the band. Tight, not his sort of music, but the drummer could play and the guitars sounded good through the venue's PA. He noticed a guy talking to the sound engineer and decided to go speak to them both on the way to the bar. Gary was a tall Irish lad with a shaved head who'd also just moved to London in search of dreams of making it big in the punk scene. He'd had the same idea as Ben and had come to the venue to meet like-minded individuals and maybe a muse who'd nosh him off. A kindred spirit thought Ben as Gary made blow job gestures with his hands. They laughed and joked while sharing stories of musical influences, favourite albums and the like. Gary was a nice guy and a potential mate but was too different in his musical tastes to work with in a band. Almost like Stu from back home, who Ben realised he hadn't told. Excusing his anti-social behaviour Ben text messaged Stu and felt he could now get on with tonight.

"My round, what you having?" Ben said standing up. He pulled his wallet out of his pocket to get a note out and nearly dropped the wraps of heroin that were in there on the floor. "Shit" he thought to himself and panicked. He didn't want people he didn't know seeing those and assuming things about him so he decided the best course of action would be to go to the toilet and flush them before going to the bar and ordering the beers. Making his way to the toilets at the back he became distracted by what he would term an impeccable arse stood at the bar. First looking down then up past the arse again he saw a swathe of strawberry blonde hair. Forgetting instantly about his heroin dilemma he began making his way over.

"I already like this town," he thought to himself.

# Chapter 14

Staring out the window at the statue of Pope Pius on the church opposite and noticing it was starting to look like winter outside, Karl barely registered that his Chemistry lesson had finished and everyone was packing up. He was meant to be going straight to the 'Sheaf after college for a pint with Martin and the lads but had now decided he couldn't be bothered. To be quite frank just his own company was going to be enough today, especially after the massive argument he and Helen had had last night. She'd ignored his texts all day too and wasn't outside the library with all her friends when he went to look for her. He'd resigned himself to the fact it was probably over for good this time. All because he'd got his days mixed up and had stayed in when he should have gone out with her and her friends on a double date last night. It was a genuine mistake but when she'd accused him of getting stoned or joyriding with Martin and his mates instead, he'd flown off the handle and now he'd lost her. What a dickhead!

He wasn't in the mood for talking to anyone on the bus either so making his excuses he braved the cold and the bracing wind as he turned left up Cambridge Road and decided to walk home. Alone with his thoughts he popped into the Trawl for a quick pint, drinking it slowly as he thought about Helen and how he always seemed intent on ruining a good thing for himself. Swilling the last mouthful round the bottom of the glass before swallowing it and watching the foam slide down the glass sides, he pondered getting another. The barmaid smiled after catching him looking at the bottom of the glass.

"You won't find any answers down there you know."

"Aye but I might forget the question."

"Fuck me I'm turning into me Dad," Karl thought as he decided against the next drink and fastened up his coat to brave the elements once more. It was bitter on Littlecoates Road as he passed the church. As he approached the grass verge onto Mayfair Drive, he noticed a familiar friendly face in a Healing uniform sat on the bus stop bench looking pensive and close to tears.

"Cheer up Hannah it might never happen."

"Alright Karlos long time no see."

"Yeah I know, who you getting to do your homework nowadays?"

"Cheeky sod!"

"Why the long face Han Solo, what's wrong?"

Hannah broke down in tears and replied "everything, errr nothing."

Karl sat down beside Hannah and gave her a big hug. He'd fantasised about feeling her boobs pressing against him for so long but had never imagined it would happen in this scenario. The tears rolling down her face stemming the blood flow to his cock as he tried his hardest not to get erect.

"Come on kiddo, come back to mine for a brew and you can tell me all about it if you want."

Normally, he'd stop in the Jube to check in on his Dad but thought better of it as Hannah could probably do without everyone's letchy comments today. Karl watched her cross the road in front of him. She'd lost a bit of her puppy fat from her arse and her boobs looked a bit bigger, if that was possible. Plus she'd be 16 now. If it wasn't for Helen, and of course Macca, he definitely still would and he sure as hell would not feel guilty when he was wanking himself off to her tonight.

Unlocking the door and nearly falling over today's post Karl made his way into the kitchen and filled the kettle, trying his best to get Hannah to speak as he waited for it to boil. Hannah looked at Karl as he stirred the milk into the tea. He had such a kind face. Taking her coat off she was careful her shirt sleeves didn't ride too high. It was one thing talking about feeling sad, it was another having to explain the cuts and cigarette burns. They chatted away with Hannah explaining the bare minimum she could so that Karl knew she had been poorly but not think she was a complete headcase. Christ nobody except her mum, not even Gemma, knew the full extent of how truly ill she was. Mild bipolar disorder, manic depression, was what the psychiatrist had called it but she knew she wasn't crazy. She knew it was mainly down to her feelings for him and what she perceived he had done.

Finishing their tea she asked to borrow a cigarette, Karl offered pulled the fags, Rizlas and a bag of weed out - "I can do better than that," he said as he constructed the familiar L-shape with the skins. They went outside under the car porch, laughing and joking about teachers, joint friends and the latest series of This Morning with Richard Not Judy. Hannah was freezing but genuinely enjoying herself for the first time in a long while actually laughing at Karl's poor impressions. As he passed the joint to her Hannah caught Karl looking at her cold stiffened nipples and realised something. It was something that no amount of prescriptions for green and yellow fluoxetine capsules or pink propranolol tablets or the lithium or even benzodiazepines, and certainly no amount of talking to barely qualified counsellors with Arts degrees would ever put right. She needed to be wanted. She wanted to be needed. She craved attention, and she craved love.

"Can I have a hug please Karl?"

Holding Karl close she used her breasts as weapons as she pushed them into him, feeling him respond and sensing his stiffening cock on her stomach. Pushing away she kissed him slowly as she massaged his cock and balls through his Levis jeans. Dropping to her knees she began unbuckling and unbuttoning him in the car porch as she sucked for all her worth.

"Let's go inside," he said.

∆ ∆ ∆

With his dick buried in Hannah's ample cleavage Karl felt the warmth building in the base of his cock. Much as he wanted to cover her boobs in cum he slowed down and changed position. He'd wanted this for far too long and wanted to savour it, not have it over and done within seconds. He lay her down and licked, kissed and nibbled every inch of her body, taking care not to dwell too long of the areas of fresh scarring on her arms and legs to avoid any embarrassing and abrupt halts to proceedings. Inhaling her scent he began licking and sucking her clitoris until he sent her into a shuddering orgasm, then making her get on all fours he hungrily ate her anus and teased her clit with his fingers, carrying on until hot liquid pumped out of her now throbbing and pulsating pussy down her thighs and onto the mattress. Adjusting position she got Karl to lie on his back, teased him with her hands to full erection and slowly guided him into her before riding him slowly, building up speed gradually. She grabbed his hands and guided them to her throat.

"Choke me Karl," she said

Karl placed his hands around her throat and squeezed lightly. Placing her hands on his....

"I SAID FUCKING CHOKE ME!"

Karl squeezed harder until Hannah's face turned red.

"HARDER!!"

Hannah's lips turned blue as she gyrated herself to orgasm, her juices running out and over Karl's balls. She proceeded to get back on all fours and Karl obliged. Spanking and doing her hard from behind, squeezing her nipples, he brought her to orgasm once more then couldn't quite work out if she was moaning in pleasure or crying as he pumped his seed deep inside her. Collapsing and kissing her back as she whispered....

"God, I've missed you Tim."

Removing his spent cock angrily Karl heard the metacarpal crack as he broke his hand punching the wall while leaving the room, slamming the door behind him. Hannah lay in his bed naked, sobbing and with his semen oozing out of her. He sat on the toilet listening to Hannah's sobs as she got dressed and ran downstairs out of the house, picking up his phone and texting Helen "I'm sorry x."

# Chapter 15

Vikki looked in the mirror as she straightened her long strawberry blonde hair. She didn't want to go out tonight at all, she was knackered from studying and working extra shifts on the bank to help get some money. She looked around her bedroom for a reasonably clean bra and put it on, now just to decide what to wear. Michelle, her flatmate, had insisted they all go tonight and meet her new boyfriend at one of his band's gigs. That was one of the best things about studying at Kings, she'd managed to wangle a room in the nurses accommodation at Guy's and St. Thomas' hospital so not only did it mean living in London was semi affordable it also meant she had people other from her course mates to socialise with. Deciding on a green top which accentuated her strawberry blonde hair and her new Top Shop jeans, which were very tight around her arse, she looked in the mirror once more. Turning, she admired her bum and thought it was definitely her best asset, secretly hoping someone there might notice it tonight and mean not another night alone with her rampant rabbit trying to muffle its noises with the duvet.

Vikki sat down in the living room area of their flat to put her shoes on as Michelle poured her an exceptionally large glass of Chardonnay and they chatted about work and guys whilst waiting for their other flatmates Paula and Mercy to finish getting ready, one of whom, probably Paula, was still in the shower. Vikki swilled the wine around the glass mimicking the guy from the wine tasting day they'd had the other week - "I'm getting apples and strawberries, what nose are you getting Michelle?"

"Cardboard and foil and cheap plonk."

A few glasses later and Vikki had an unmistakable glow in her face and a warm desire in her knickers as she felt the effects of the carton wine, yet they were still waiting for Paula. She decided to go out to the cashpoint and shops while everyone else waited. Exiting Orchard Lisle House onto Talbot Yard she went through the little alleyway that opened up to a busy generic, yet unmistakably London, road. Doing her errands and smoking two cigarettes to the filter before going back upstairs to Mercy in a tight and short red dress showing a lot of leg. Paula eventually joining them, sipping her wine and pulling her ridiculously tall heels on. For what was meant to be a relatively quiet night out, the girls were drinking hard and the three singletons were dressed to kill.

"How we getting there?"
"It's only 2 stops on the tube."
"In these heels?!"
"Good point."
"There is 4 of us let's just get a cab."

In the back of the cab Vikki found herself shifting her stare from Paula's heels to Mercy's long black legs in her mini dress then to Michelle's clearly stiff nipples in a top that made it obvious she wasn't wearing a bra. She'd never had these sorts of desires about girls before but she could feel the gusset of her panties becoming very damp as she fantasised about all three of her flatmates. "Tonight I must get laid" she thought for the third or fourth or more probably ninth time today and right now she didn't care if it was by a male or female or anything in between.

The club was dark, dingy and smoke filled. It reminded Vikki of Gullivers but with live music. They found a table and Vikki watched Mercy's bum as she went to get drinks, trying not to look too hungrily in case she got caught. God, Mercy had a nice bottom, it looked, she thought narcissistically, almost as good as hers. The band had already started, Michelle's boyfriend on drums - he was cute with nice hair. The band were actually very good a psychedelic edge and all in time but the singer looked like an anorexic girl and sounded like he was in pain. This was not helped by his make-up that he was inexplicably wearing. Mercy's round soon disappeared into the thirsty girl's stomachs so Vikki got up to go to the bar deciding shooters were in order alongside the regular long drinks. She stood at the bar trying to get the server's attention when a voice came from behind her.

"Of all the gin bars in all the world."

Vikki didn't turn around because she didn't know if she'd be ridiculously angry or would look stupid with the smile she now had on her face and simply replied

"It's gin joints Ben."

She felt his hands on her waist so she turned round to face him. Just as good looking as she remembered her stomach was full of butterflies. She wanted to ask why he hadn't bothered speaking to her for over two years and why he thought better of it tonight but her primal urges got the better of her. Besides no man she'd been with since had made her cum like he had that night and the rabbit was a poor substitute. He went in for a kiss but she coyly turned her head and let him peck her on the cheek, it was going to be easy but he didn't need to know just how easy yet.

Ben pulled a seat up with Vikki and her friends and she had to try hard to keep his attention from wandering off her to her flat mates, surprising herself by rubbing his thigh when she caught him checking out Mercy's sexy legs. Chatting about the music Michelle's boyfriend came over when his band had finished. Ben and Scott chatted and were getting along very well, Michelle had mentioned to Vikki that Scott was a bisexual and he was flirting incessantly with Ben. How dare he? How dare he do that to Michelle while she was sat there? How dare she do it to her with her man?!

The next band on were a reasonably good indie guitar band and Scott and Ben got up to listen closer, Scott clearly still flirting and Ben, now a little tipsy, reciprocating. Michelle noticed Vikki's annoyance and slid over to speak to her.

"I was going to let Scott suck him off while I watched but I can see you like him a lot."

"He's just a friend."

"That maybe so but you want more, it's obvious."

Vikki felt herself going redder than her hair, she thought she'd been playing it cool but apparently not. Scott and Ben came back, so she grabbed Ben's hand to squeeze it just so he knew. Ben knew alright and smiled a smile which sent electricity into Vikki's pants which must have been obvious as she shuffled her legs making Ben's hungry eyes open wider and his tongue touch his teeth.

The final band of the night were 4 female singers with a keyboard. Very different to the other bands that had been on and Vikki overheard Scott and Ben mumbling about promoters not knowing their audiences but didn't really catch it all nor care as she was still holding Ben's hand. During the fourth song the couples called it a night and go back to the flat in the nurses accommodation leaving Mercy and Paula behind to try and find some male company.

In the taxi Ben held Vikki's hand with his right hand, fingers entwined and starting the foreplay while the fingers on his left hand were in his pocket doing similar to the wraps of heroin he still hadn't disposed of. Back at the flat another carton of Chardonnay was opened and flowed very quickly, Ben and Vikki's hands grabbing any opportunity to touch. As the carton emptied, excuses were made as everybody went to their respective rooms. In Vikki's room a long kiss ensued as Ben and Vikki slowly, yet hungrily, undressed each other, teasing skin with touches and kisses until, finally naked, Ben lay Vikki down and kissed down her stomach until he reached her now soaking pussy. Licking slowly yet intently he brought Vikki to a climax she had not felt since the last time she was in bed with Ben as the urgency waved over her spot and her pussy contracted covering his face in her juices. Moving up and guiding his huge member into her they made love until the sun rose, her climaxing almost constantly.

Shielding his eyes as the bright October sun crept through the crack in the curtains on to his face Ben looked down at the head of strawberry blonde hair snoozing on his shoulder and felt at ease for the first time. He pecked the top of her head with a kiss.

"Morning."
"What time is it?" Vikki asked wearily
"Just gone 8."
"Is it Monday?"
"Yeah."
"Shit I've got lectures!"

Watching Vikki pull a black lace thong around her impeccable arse Ben heard himself say something he'd never thought he would as he asked for her number. Her heart skipped a beat, and she got uncontrollable butterflies in her stomach. She stumbled over the order of a 3 and a 7 and repeated her number an embarrassing four times to make sure he'd definitely got the right one. He repeated it to her so she was satisfied he had although she had a deep down worry the phone would never beep and Ben would be out of her life and she'd be back to her life of disappointing sex or her vibrator.

Ben's mind was everywhere as he left the digs to walk to the underground and make his way back to his bedsit, once again going the wrong way on the tube 2 stops before realising. He really needed to learn how this bloody thing worked! When he eventually found his place, he made a brew then sat down on the floor and picked up his guitar. Strumming a G he realised it was horribly out of tune so he tuned up by ear then strummed a satisfying chord. Mind still racing he removed his phone and wallet from his pockets and strummed another G but he still couldn't concentrate.

Placing the guitar down he went over to his jacket and removed his cigarettes and lighter, repositioned himself on the floor with his guitar and lit a cigarette. Strumming a G then a D he tapped the ash on the floor and then found himself doing something he'd never done before for the second time in as many hours by picking up his phone and texting Vikki.

HAD A GR8 NYT. CAN I C U AGAIN?

He took the opportunity to delete Dave's number then placed the phone back down in front of him, hoping the message alert would shrill soon. Brain hurting from a lack of sleep and a little hungover he finished the cigarette. Stubbing it out on the floor tiles he made a mental note to steal an ashtray from the pub. He then strummed the same pattern over again, G then D, G then D as a melody entered but quickly left his head. He idly lit the lighter and blew it out three times, then placed his guitar down, opened up his wallet, took out a wrap and went to the bin to remove the meticulously folded Kit-Kat foil.

# Chapter 16

Bobby finished his pint and watched the foam sink down as he once again looked for the poignant answers that weren't ever forthcoming. It had been that long he wasn't sure there were even any relevant questions any more, just that there definitely wasn't any answers. Rising from his usual seat in the Jubilee he stood swaying, catching his balance before making his way to the gents. Washing his face in the sink he took a long, hard look at himself in the mirror. He had a greyish yellowish pallor except for the broken veins around his nose which was becoming more and more crimson. He dragged a comb across his greying hair before going to relieve himself at the urinal. Looking down at the bright yellow trickle slowly dripping out of his withered lifeless cock burning his urethra with a dull fire he knew he should get seen to.

"BASTARD!" He shouted at nobody as he put himself away before the last of his urine had evacuated his bladder causing a big wet patch on his best slacks. He went over and grabbed some paper towels before trying his best to dry himself on the fart of warm air emanating from the electric hand dryer. Deciding he'd done the best he could do, he returned to the bar noticing for the first time a group of giggling girls playing pool who were clearly the topic of conversation between Paul, John and Steve the landlord.

"It's like a fucking crèche in here tonight."

"Not much I can do about it John, they've all got ID."

"Aye and you like 'em young don't you?"

"What the fuck is that supposed to mean?"

"Nothing Steve."

All four of them knew exactly what it was supposed to mean but nobody was in the mood for the fight or being barred from their local boozer so the conversation halted abruptly. It wasn't the first time Steve had been accused and it probably wouldn't be the last. He had a reputation of being easy to get served in his bars and the pub had "pedo" graffitied on it several times a year. Nothing had ever happened as far as the police getting involved so Bobby assumed it was just malicious rumours and went about his business, it hadn't affected him and the Jube was a convenient stagger away from home and it served alcohol. Although he did always think that there was no smoke without fire and if you flung enough shit some of it would stick. Paying for his drink Bobby sat back down in his usual spot, chair moulded to his arse cheeks after years of use, to see if maybe this pint had his answers.

∆ ∆ ∆

Gemma, Lindsey and Cheryl were out in the Jube playing pool. Gemma felt guilty for not inviting Hannah but she'd been a bit weird recently and she didn't know Lindsey very well so didn't have the fake ID her brother Phil sold. They didn't normally need it in the Jube, just a flash of your cleavage and a flirtatious smile at the landlord and you was alright but the woman had served them tonight so they were thankful of them. Nobody had ever tried one of Phil's fake ID cards out in Town or Cleethorpes but they were accepted at the Jube, Wisebuy and Victoria Wine so booze and fags weren't too much of a problem as long as you were staying on the estate. The snooty cow in McColls wouldn't accept it though but rumour was that it's because Phil never made her one when she was at school with him.

Gemma saw the old pissheads looking over at them and decided she'd tease them by deliberately bending over so her arse or cleavage was pointing at them. It got her the attention she so desperately craved and she wondered if her reputation had been picked up by the older generation or not, secretly hoping so as it turned her on. Testing the water she went over to John and Paul.

"Hi guys, I'm Gemma, that's Lindsey, and that's Cheryl, now which one of you gorgeous gentlemen would like to buy us a drink?"

Lindsey and Cheryl were giggling nervously, mortified that she could be so brazen. They were slightly less mortified when Gemma returned with 6 bottles of alcopop and the two elder alcoholics in tow. Cheryl laughed as she wondered what the suffragettes would say about Gemma using her femininity to great use coercing increasingly more booze out of the guys and even convincing them to pay for the pool table too. Gemma flirted incorrigibly with Paul as John seemed more interested in his beer than her boobs anyway, she thought he must either be a puff or too much alcohol over the years had numbed his cock beyond the point of no return.

At 10 o'clock the elderly looking guy who'd been sat on his own watching them said goodbye and Gemma realised it was Karl's Dad who she met before her first threesome a couple of years ago, swiftly followed by Cheryl and Lindsey who both had to be home earlier than her. Pretty soon there was only her and Paul playing pool as John, tired of childish prattle and paying for drinks, had returned to putting the world to rights with Steve. Paul was never very good at pool and was about to leave Gemma to it when she turned to him and said

"Paul, go get us another couple of drinks while I set up the balls and if you beat me, I'll give you a blow job."

Paul's cock, which had seen no action at all in the 90s sprang to so much attention it nearly broke his trouser's fly and you could have played pool with it itself. He practically ran to the bar hoping somehow he could win a game of pool for once - if the world was coming to an end because of the Millennium Bug with planes falling out the sky and all the computers crashing then he sure as hell needed sucking off by a 16-year-old before it happened.

Paul downed his first pint then broke the triangle of balls sending them flying in all directions across the table. Checking out Gemma's arse as she bent over to play her shot his normally lifeless cock was twitching. He'd always been uncomfortable around women and was much happier with a pint in his hand anyway. Gemma missed what should have been an easy shot and Paul hoped it was deliberate and she was going easy on him because she wanted him to win. A guy could hope couldn't he?

As Gemma potted one of Paul's reds instead of her easy yellow, she looked at him and said:

"Fuck the game of pool, get in the beer garden."

Nervously following her outside, Paul couldn't believe his luck. His cock was throbbing as she pushed him into the corner and got down on her knees, unbuckling his belt. Paul, eager to break the awkward silence and to reaffirm that this was actually happening struggled for the words to say. In a quivering, almost breaking voice he softly said:

"Do you like my pants? They're new."

"Fuck the pants" Gemma said as she unleashed his rock hard cock and took it down her throat in one go. Hungrily lapping at his bell end and Jap's eye. Paul grabbed a handful of her hair and started to fuck her mouth. Building up a rhythm that felt good in his balls.

"You dirty bastards!" Steve shouted catching them in the act

"You're only jealous. Tell you what let me finish then I'll give you one too."

"I don't think so you slag. You're both barred."

"What's the matter? Aren't I young enough for you?"

"What the fuck did you say, you slaggy little cunt?"

"You heard you fucking sick paedo."

"FUCKING SLAG!"

Steve saw red and ran over towards Gemma, knocking her flying and smashing her cheekbone with a large right haymaker. She screamed on the floor crying. Paul, trousers around his knees, cock still erect, defending his lady's honour swung a punch-cum-push at Steve which was easily dodged as Steve swung a right at Paul knocking him to the ground too. There was a sickening thud accompanied by a scream as Steve stamped his foot down on Paul's skull.

"FUCKING CUNT!"

Going back inside, throwing John out and locking the doors, hands shaking from the adrenaline, Steve got some ice for his bruised knuckles and filled a glass with whisky from the optics. Paul was laid in a bloody mess as John helped him up, Gemma long gone Paul planned his revenge.

# Chapter 17

Thinking about what a shit time he was having at the moment and how well he'd kept his anger in check recently Macca got ready for his run. Yes he was still involved in the territorial escapades that the football offered him but that was becoming less frequent. In running he had really found a coping mechanism that was successfully keeping him in gainful employment and out of jail. He needed to keep out of trouble with the police as he was on his final warning with the courts for his violent behaviour and one copper in particular, Hughes, seemed to have a vendetta against him. His court appointed solicitor had suggested taking up exercise. He'd tried boxing, but that made him more violent when people hit him, plus he couldn't hide his erection in the shorts they'd given him. Then he tried the gym but the posers there in their designer gear flexing their muscles in the mirrors had made him angry and it turned out that lifting weights just didn't float his boat. But in a pair of trackie bottoms and trainers pounding the streets of Grimsby or the promenade with his earphones in, late at night, he felt at ease and could forget about the images of pummeling his boss's head into the wall or worrying about which of the town's many reprobates wanted to impregnate any of his sisters. Not that he had shown it to anyone, but he was particularly worried about his youngest sister Hannah who was really going through a messy time and had seemed to withdraw into herself.

Tonight's route was a quick 5 mile round trip round Cleethorpes up Taylor's Ave, he could easily do 15 miles and he had even thought about entering himself for the marathon and raising some money for charity. Setting off as a light jog he upped the pace as he forgot about the entire world except him, his music and the road.

∆ ∆ ∆

They'd seen them arguing in the pub earlier and when she stormed out, they'd taken a gamble on her coming this way and it had paid off - they were overjoyed she was now in sight again. They'd passed them on the street arguing and now they waited in the bush on their own, balaclava already on, slowly stroking their phallus as they watched them arguing at the top of the path. The boyfriend was really angry and she was wearing a short skirt so was practically begging for it the little slag. The boyfriend stormed off leaving her alone in the park and walking towards the bushes where they waited - "come on now slag not long now" they thought as she staggered in their direction. Slipping the condom on and then their gloves they knew that her time had come. Grabbing her, hand over the mouth, they punched the back of her head and dragged her into the bush. Lifting up her slaggy short skirt they tore her knickers off and violently penetrated her from behind. God, they'd forgotten how good this made them feel as their knees trembled in ecstasy.

∆ ∆ ∆

"Think this is one for you" The editor said to Neil as the police contacted the Telegraph. Neil had ran several stories on the beast's return two years ago but, just like in 1992, the rapes had just appeared to stop as quickly as they started. Now it seemed as though the beast had struck again, a little further out than usual in Haverstoe Park but all the usual hallmarks. Picking up the phone he called Morris at the police station to get as much information as he could, which as always was practically none. No witnesses, no real evidence, no DNA. Neil wondered how many times he could rehash the same story and just change the location and the number of victims but then felt guilty as he thought about the poor victims and their families. Then, strangely, even more guilt arose in his stomach as he thought about the police who were trying to catch an invisible man. He pondered his story with precision as he daydreamed of this eventually catapulting him to bigger things in the national press or even television.

Disagreeing with the editor how best to report this they settled with the headline "Return of the Beast?" even though this made Neil guiltily sing the Mark Morrison song in his head. Printing the e-fit images that were still, despite technological advances, just a pair of generic colourless eyes in a badly drawn balaclava alongside the incident room number appealing for witnesses.

∆ ∆ ∆

Pete shouted through to Ethel to get him the paper as he heard the paperboy push the evening edition through the door. Ethel was busy cooking tea and told him to get it himself. Groaning he stood up and went through to the hall and picked up the paper. Turning it to the back page "Bloody Town - lost 5-2 to Charlton, that's 3 on the trot now" he grumbled at his beloved club's misfortunes. He remembered back to the 1939 semi-final at Old Trafford and how the kids today would never probably experience that, but, by all accounts, this Buckley bloke had got them playing some good stuff and they held their own. At 83 his legs weren't what they were, so he didn't get to go to Blundell Park as much as he liked, if at all, and, for some reason, he hadn't had his Sports Telegraph delivered again this Saturday. He must take that up with the guy at the shop. He hobbled back to his chair and read the match report tutting occasionally as he read about the Mariners' latest defeat. Turning to the front page he shouted through "Bloody 'ell Eth that beast is back" as he read the page aloud. Ethel dropped the pan and said:

"What was the name of that lad who used to knock about with our Mike? You know, crazy kid, always trouble around him, McDonald or something wasn't it?"

"The football yobbo? Mac something yeah, Mac, erm......they all called him Macca I think, why Eth?"

"I see him running dead fast away from the park last night."

"Best phone the cops our Eth, just in case."

∆ ∆ ∆

The buzz around Grimsby nick was electric as word spread they'd got a lead at last. An eye witness seeing someone running away and a name. A name most of them knew. Lucas was ecstatic when he found out the name was MacKenzie, the football hooligan who'd embarrassed him the other year, the one he'd been after for months. That bastard would get his comeuppance and Lucas smugly smiled as he hatched a plan to make sure he was there to watch it in all its Technicolour glory.

# Chapter 18

Exhausted after yet another session of multiple climaxes Vikki rolled off the top of Ben to his side to give him a post coital cuddle. He moved away quickly reaching for the ashtray before laying back down with it on his chest and passing her a cigarette.

They'd been a proper item for three months and this was a different Ben to the womaniser she first met and knew back in Grimsby. He'd definitely changed and if it was possible, the sex just kept getting better and better - although the last few times his mind had seemed to be elsewhere. She knew he was worried - he'd not had any sign of a gig since moving to London and she was concerned for his mental well-being. He'd given up everything to move, and she thought he might be struggling with money. He'd sold his guitar and bought a cheaper one to make ends meet and she was certain he wasn't eating properly. Nuzzling into his shoulders she noticed he seemed to be losing weight and her caring instincts kicked in as she thought she must concentrate more on looking after her man and cooking him some meals. She felt guilty because she knew he'd pulled out the stops to romance her and now he was struggling the romance had all but disappeared and she didn't like it. She hadn't expected it to last forever but Jesus he had even started leaving his bloody socks on in bed. Was this all her fault for accusing him of sleeping with Mercy the other week? She hadn't meant to but there was definitely chemistry between them and she'd caught him looking at her legs on more than one occasion. Plus he'd been talking in his sleep about his beautiful brown angel and as far as she knew Mercy was the only girl he knew who'd fit the bill.

She stubbed the cigarette out into the ashtray and kissed his shoulders hugging him tightly and nearly spilling the contents of the overflowing ashtray over him. She wanted to tell him she loved him but didn't want to frighten him off, he'd only just committed to a monogamous relationship with someone for the first time in his life so he might not be ready for the dreaded "three words" just yet and might run a mile. She kissed him once more and decided on “I really enjoy spending time with you.” He grunted an inaudible response which all but confirmed his mind was elsewhere. She wanted to confront him about his attitude but didn’t want to argue and risk losing him. Laying there in confusion and exhausted from another sex session she drifted off in his arms.

∆ ∆ ∆

Looking at her strawberry blonde mane asleep on his shoulder Ben contemplated how the hell he could move her without waking her and get to what he really needed in the bathroom cabinet. He’d wanted her to leave after they’d finished but thought better of asking her to go. After all his feelings for her were only eclipsed by the contents of that bag in the bathroom. He’d never ever in his life felt feelings like he felt for these two things. Was he in love with Vikki? Yes, probably, almost certainly, but he couldn’t tell her, especially while she still lived with Mercy. Even if it wasn’t love she was definitely different to all the other girls, and he hadn’t slept with another girl since their first date, even when Mercy had all but offered him it on a plate he'd politely declined out of respect for Vikki. He'd avoided going back to their place since Vikki had accused him of sleeping with Mercy. He hadn't fucked her but he sure as hell would do and knew that he could. He'd never had a black girl before and wondered if it was any different and if the saying once you'd had black you don't go back only counted for women. Thinking about her long legs and black nipples stirred his loins and for a split second he wanted to wake Vikki up for another session but his balls ached from their recent marathons and he had other pressing matters.

Some lyrics came into his head so he grabbed his pad and pen off the bedroom table and scribbled them down, almost resenting Vikki being by his side as he couldn't pick up his guitar and write the melody too. Lighting another cigarette he longingly looked at the bathroom door hoping he'd be alone with his other love soon. He text Scott about having a jam later in the week and about getting a gig together. If nothing else he needed the cash pretty sharpish plus the whole point in being in London was to get his music heard and that had seemed to have taken a back burner to his other extra-curricular activities. Scott text back asking about tonight but Ben already had made his plans. He just needed to get shot of Vikki.

ΔΔΔ

Vikki woke up still on Ben's shoulder, she was pleased to see he was writing which meant he had got some motivation for his music for the first time in a while. She knew she had to think it because of their relationship, but he really was a good singer and an excellent songwriter and she was certain if he put his mind to it like he'd come down to London to do then he could make it. She wondered for a while if she was holding him back with their relationship but then thought that Ben definitely knew his own mind and would surely have said something if he didn't want her to be there. Maybe that's why his mind had been elsewhere, maybe he'd been thinking about his music more recently and he was in his own world. Maybe that's just what he was like, after all apart from the unreal, incredible sex she didn't really know much else about him.

She playfully bit Ben's nipple and he responded by lifting her up so that they could kiss. Fingers wandering he teased her to the brink of climax - but once again it was obvious, his mind was on something else and Vikki couldn't quite just let herself tip over the edge. Eventually, due to his persistence, Vikki shuddered, moaning in pleasure on Ben's skillful fingers. She composed herself, then bit the bullet and asked him what was wrong.

"Nothing why?"

"You seem to be elsewhere."

"Sorry, no I'm not, sorry," he lied

"No Ben I'm sorry I shouldn't have said anything, is it your music?"

"Erm, yeah, sort of."

"Do you want me to leave you to it tonight?"

"You don't have to," he said secretly hoping she would.

"No baby I will, if you've got a song you want to work on the last thing you need is me here."

Not believing his luck and mind racing elsewhere Ben shocked himself and Vikki as he said

"Thank you, I love you."

"Wow Ben, really? Wow, err, I love you too" her heart melted as butterflies erupted in her stomach and she kissed him more passionately than she had kissed anyone ever before. Ben then found himself even further from his usual self as he made love to Vikki strictly in the missionary position, slowly, thoughtfully, passionately, lovingly kissing all the way through. Orgasming together they carried on kissing until Ben had gone limp inside Vikki.

"Right I'll leave you to it" Vikki said as she pulled on her clothes leaving Ben in bed naked apart from his socks. "Those fucking socks" she thought as she looked back pondering how to approach him about them and get them gone as she closed the door behind her and made her way back to her flat to actually do some studying for a change.

Within seconds of the door closing Ben was in the bathroom cabinet taking out his wash bag and inspecting the contents. He needed to get more soon, and he definitely needed a new needle as this one was getting blunt. Measuring out the heroin on the spoon, adding the citric acid and then a syringe full of tap water he heated it slowly until everything was as dissolved as it could be. This stuff wasn't as good or as soluble as copper Dave's but all that had long gone and this was the only gear he'd managed to get his hands on in London so far. Drawing it up through an unused cigarette filter he tapped the syringe and expelled the air bubble like the dealer had shown him. Removing his right sock he carefully examined the previous needle marks as he found a vein, painfully piercing his skin with the barbed needle, drawing back then plunging the syringe fully. The warmth spread over his body as he drifted off to his private oblivion, laying partially comatose on the cold bathroom floor.

# Chapter 19

Another night shift and yet another shift having to put up with Davies was not what the doctor had ordered for Lucas today. Davies had been grumpier than usual over the last 3 months ever since going to that empty flat on Welholme Road. Tonight seemed much worse, everything was "bastard this" or "bastard that" which usually would have offended Lucas but today he could have quite happily joined in. That little sod Macca had been released without charge earlier basically because whichever incompetent prick who couldn't find their arse with their truncheon had failed to uncover any evidence and the victim didn't pick him out in the ID parade with either the balaclava on or not. No DNA and no identification in the parade made it very difficult to make the arrest. Lucas took solace that his cards were marked now and every copper in Grimsby would be watching his moves to make sure he couldn't satisfy his disgusting urges, especially Morris the lead detective who Lucas had a lot of respect for. One of the last good guys cut from the same cloth as him.

They pulled out the station and headed out of town towards the telegraph flyover. Lucas automatically assuming that Davies wanted to go visit one of his Eastern European friends at Nicole's but Dave wasn't in the mood for that instead directing Lucas the other way out of town towards the industrial estate.

Pulling off the A180 at Great Coates roundabout they pulled in a car full of young lads and took the opportunity to remind them that the road between Great Coates and Healing was a 40 zone and not a race track. They then went and surprised a young couple, telling them that the lay-by on the same stretch of road possibly wasn't the best place to get amorous, but only after watching for a few minutes. Davies mentioning the young girl had a "nice pair of tits" while Lucas noticed the guy was cute and had a perfect cock which was about 8 inches and straight, smooth and very very suckable. Letting them both off with a slap on the wrists the two policemen drove off and headed towards the Wybers.

Turning right onto Wybers Way they saw an orange glow at the top of the hill and realised that the Jubilee was on fire. Lucas hit the lights and sped up whilst Davies called the incident in. The fire must have only just started as no members of the public had yet reported it and the flames were relatively small. Looking in through the window as best and as safely as he could Lucas could not see any people inside. He was knocked off his feet by the explosion of the gas bottles in the cellar, sent flying a good ten feet backwards by the force. Dave, in between fits of laughter from the sight, ambled over to check on his partner. Slightly bruised, his ego more than his coccyx, Lucas stood up shakily.

"Think we're best waiting for the brigade" Dave said to him stifling his childish giggles, secretly glad no harm had come to Lucas. Imagine the bloody paperwork if it had he thought, plus he wasn't a bad kid, just a bit eager and a bit of an arse licker.

Two fire engines sped up Wybers Way and blocked the mini roundabout to the whole estate. Morris sped behind them screeching to a halt perpendicular to the kerb, waking the majority of residents who had not already assembled to have a good gander at what was going on. The centre of Wybers, awash with colour from the fire and blue lights looking like Lincolnshire's version of the Northern Lights at 2 in the morning as the local busy bodies and feral kids gathered round passing their immense firefighting expertise on to the clear amateurs of Humberside Fire Service as Lucas, Davies and Morris tried their best, albeit unsuccessfully, to keep the crowd back and let the firemen get on with putting out the local pub.

Out of the corner of his eye Dave saw two faces he recognised as new drinkers in the Valiant watching intently as the inferno raged and the firemen struggled to contain it. He thought to himself that there was going to be a lot more new drinkers in there soon now this place was gone and was caught in a dilemma as to whether or not this was a good thing. The downside was that there might be a struggle for seats as the new invaders from the Wybers landed but on a positive note, new faces meant new opportunities for business.

As the flames turned to embers the crowd, disappointed at not seeing the pub razed to the ground, dissipated and left the fire brigade and the police there to finish their jobs. On the soot stained front wall of the Jube in bright yellow paint, crudely scrawled, were the words “PEEDO NONCE CUNT” and “FUCKING PERVERT”.

Morris looked at Davies and Lucas and asked if they knew if there was anyone who might have a vendetta against the landlord. Both replied to the negative, although Dave had heard the rumours about Steve he never thought they would be true. He’d always assumed it was something a disgruntled ex drinker with a personal axe to grind had made up to make him look bad, but thinking on he had never seen Steve with a bird and one of the girls at Nicole’s had told him he liked a shaved cunt so maybe there was some truth.

"I reckon we're dealing with an arson here lads," said Lucas.

"No fucking flies on you" Dave retorted in a lairy tone.

His suspicions confirmed as a fireman returned from inside the building carrying a jerry can which had clearly been used to start the fire.

# Chapter 20

"Your round mate" Ian turned to Ben and said.

"Bloody hell mate we've only just got the last ones in. You thirsty?"

"I'm drier than a Nun's cunt mate, may as well get a jug."

Saturday afternoon drinking in Delius in front of Jeff Stelling and Soccer Saturday on the big screen had taken a back seat recently as Ian and Rosie's relationship was blossoming, but today she'd gone out shopping in Leeds with her housemates and, although it was Sunday, Grimsby vs Norwich was the 1 o'clock kick off live on Sky so they were back on it and it appeared Ian was fully intending on making the most of it by ordering a 4 pint jug. Tim, although only half way through his first pint duly obliged and got up to go to the bar. Flirting with the barmaid Tim felt a twinge in his pants and he realised he'd not had sex for over two months when he was off his head with that girl from back home with massive boobs who he'd had a wet dream on her back and she thought he was crazy. He thought about asking the barmaid for her number then realised although she was a flirt she was far too skinny and he was sure he'd seen her with a boyfriend anyway, best to keep flirting and not suffer the embarrassment of being turned down yet again.

Turning his attention away from women and back to drinking and football Tim struggled to keep up with Ian who was setting a fast pace. The clock on the match indicated that it was only about 1:25 and Ian was back at the bar coming back with another 4 pint jug and shots of Aftershock. Ian clearly wanted to get messy and Tim thought back to putting him to bed on several occasions in the past. Today was probably going to be one of those days and he'd have to take the blame and explain it all to Rosie later, but that's just what mates do for each other.

In time honoured tradition Tim necked the remainder of his pint as a Lee Ashcroft shot hit the back of the net. Getting up to go to the toilet he felt the booze already affecting his legs. Buoyed by the alcohol he was probably a little too dirty in his flirting with the barmaid as he bought the next jug and Aftershocks but she seemed to like it and no harm was really done. Town finished 2-1 winners so Tim was a happy man, even more so when he and Ian started making plans for staying at his parent's Cheadle Hulme house next weekend for Stockport vs Grimsby match then out into Manchester for the evening sounded like a great way to spend time to Tim, all they'd need to do was avoid any of his and Ian's old hooligan mates as they said hello to each other on the back streets of Edgeley. This, they agreed, was probably easier said than done but sod it.

The conversation drifted to Tim's lack of conquests recently and Ian assured him he'd get him a nice Stockport girl to fire into next weekend, although all the ones that he could think of that would let "an ugly fishy bastard" go near them could hardly be described as nice. Tim, embarrassed by his lack of recent sexual prowess and mildly offended by how he'd just been described laughed it off but then hoped that Ian actually knew some girls who would, even better if they had nice big bouncy arses. Either way, his balls needed emptying or to be quite frank beggars can't be choosers so just female with a pulse would do him at this present moment in time.

Talking about everything and nothing as more jugs and shots flowed Ian had hit the wall and was now slurring his words and you could see his eyes were struggling to focus as he spoke the usual nonsense of a man with a racing mind and too much alcohol fuelling it.

"Mate, I fucking love you you fishy bastard."

"Cheers mate."

"Did you check our lottery numbers last night?"

"No mate did you?"

"No but how fucking weird would it be if we were millionaires and sat here drinking this piss instead of champagne?"

"You don't half talk some bollocks you know?"

"I know but what would you do if you had a million quid, don't tell me, go down near the Peel and get a load of hookers you dirty bastard."

"Fuck off!"

"I feel sorry for the next girl you fuck, you're gonna fire her out the room when you cum."

"Probably right."

"Did you know diarrhoea is hereditary?"

"What the fuck?"

"Yeah it runs in your jeans!"

"Fuck off, you daft cunt, it's your round."

Ian took several attempts to raise from his seat, knees weakened by alcohol, and eventually made his way to the bar opting for vodkas and coke as his stomach capacity for fizzy lager had expired. He knew doubles probably wasn't the best idea but didn't want to lose face to Tim so ordered them anyway and returned to the table for more inane conversation.

Δ Δ Δ

In one of Bradford's less salubrious curry restaurants Tim laughed as Ian, clearly over inebriated started to fall asleep in his chicken pakora.

"Can we get the main courses as takeaway mate?" He asked the waiter so not to cause too much of a scene as in this state Ian's snoring was enough to raise the dead.

Stumbling up the hill with Ian in one arm and his bag full of curry in the other a not exactly sober Tim struggled against the wind and November rain until he got to their house. A dilapidated large six bedroom Victorian terrace that just he and Ian shared reasoning that the low rent for the whole house justified not having to share with anyone else. Dragging Ian upstairs and dumping him in his bed, Tim sat down in the lounge and turned the telly on, eating his luke warm curry before rolling a big, heavily loaded, joint and lighting it.

The front door opening indicated that Rosie had returned from her shopping trip and was letting herself in with the key Ian had given her. Tim braced himself for the ensuing argument about being irresponsible and letting Ian get drunk and was surprised that a not exactly sober Rosie seemed relaxed.

“Is he in bed?”

“Yeah, sorry about that.”

“Oh don’t be sorry, he needed it, that’s the thing with me Tim I know exactly what a man needs.”

“Lucky Ian, want some of this?” He offered her the joint.

Sitting down Rosie took a large lungful before exhaling plumes of blue grey smoke adding to the haze forming around the lights in the lounge. Passing the joint between each other until it had all gone. They agreed that they may as well watch a film as Tim started to roll another.

Rosie left to go to the toilet and Tim had a good look at her big arse as she got up from the sofa. He started to wonder what fucking her doggy style would be like and felt the all to recognisable semi hard on twinging in his pants. God he needed to get laid soon.

Returning Rosie took a seat on the sofa next to Tim, their feet touching as they both reclined. Sharing another joint as they watched the film. Before long Rosie’s head was on Tims shoulder and her hand on his chest stroking gently, Tim trying his hardest to mask the raging hard on developing. Her hand wandered down and squeezed his cock.

"Err what you doing?!"

"I told you I know exactly what a man needs."

"But Ian?"

"Ian is asleep and drunk and I won't tell him," she said now wanking him in his jeans.

Tim kissed Rosie hard and a hand reached around to her big bum that he'd wanked about on more than several occasions. Undressing each other frantically until both naked Rosie positioned herself so her peachy big bum was in the air. Tim manoeuvred himself behind her and slid in.

"You don't have to worry about which hole" Rosie looked behind her and whispered seductively.

Not requiring a second invitation Tim spat on his hand and rubbed it into Rosie's ringpiece before taking his throbbing cock out of her and easing it gently into her anus.

Rosie had always liked anal and figured she knew Tim well enough to let him, plus he wasn't going to spread any stories about her because he'd look like the bastard fucking his mate's bird so she could be filthy if she wanted. She reached up and teased her own clitoris with her fingers until she orgasmed hard feeling his balls bouncing against her arse as he kneaded her buttocks. Tim obviously liked big bums. She felt his cock becoming tight.

"I know this might sound strange but I want you to cum on me rather than in me."

Tim close to ejaculation pulled out and finished all over Rosie's big buttocks. Rubbing his cum into them enthusiastically.

"Nobody finds out about this ever" Rosie said as she gathered her clothes and went for a shower before getting into bed with Ian.

∆ ∆ ∆

The pressure built in Tim's chest as he felt his shoulders being shook. So much pressure. Hard shakes on his shoulder. His chest building with the crushing pressure as a sweat entails his body, and a buzz entraps his aural systems.

Waking with a start Tim sees Macca's sneering face, His eyes demonic - crimson rubies set in a visage twisted with malevolence.

"My fucking girlfriend" - he screams in a high pitched voice as he plants a head butt on the bridge of Tim's nose raising his head again. His blood splattered face transforming in front of Tim's watery eyes into Ian.

"What the fuck?" Tim manages to scream out as the pressure builds in his chest once more and a warm sensation drifts over his whole body.

"Tim wake the fuck up." a green looking Ian is shaking him "all fucking six numbers, all fucking six, I've spoken to them already 900 grand each. We're fucking rich!"

# Chapter 21

Morris waited patiently for back up. There'd been another attack and they were going to surprise this MacKenzie bastard in his sleep and before the cocky little fucker could hide evidence or before he'd properly woken up they could have him. Why were they taking so fucking long? There was a limited window in which to get him and they were eating into it. Lighting yet another cigarette and smoking it until the acrid smell of burnt filter filled the car he cursed more and more coarsely as each sweep of the second hand indicated another wasted precious minute until the officers eventually turned up.

"Where the fuck have you been?" He reprimanded a previously excited but now frightened looking Lucas.

"Sorry sir, we errrr......."

“Don’t give me fucking excuses, let’s get this done” Morris interrupted abruptly then apologising immediately. Morris liked Hughes, he was a grovelling little shit and he was a Yorkie but he was eager and he was going to make a good detective one day soon that was for sure.

Stepping to one side as the door was forced open, Morris felt the adrenaline pump from his kidneys as he rushed up the stairs and forcefully woke Macca up. Deliberately slamming his head into the wall as he twisted his arms around his back and tightened the handcuffs in one swift motion before Macca could ready himself for the fight.

“Steven MacKenzie, I’m arresting you on suspicion of rape. You do not have to say anything but it may harm your defence if you do not mention something which you later rely on in court. Anything you do say may be given in evidence.”

“You’ve got fuck all on me just some old biddy that see us on me run.”

“We both know we’re talking about last night.”

“I was in bed all fucking night.”

“Tell me at the station.”

"I want my lawyer."

Morris escorted Macca down to the car, purposefully neglecting to place his hand over his head so that it slammed on the door frame.

"That fucking hurt and these cuffs are too tight."

"Thought you were meant to be a tough guy." Morris sneered before turning to Lucas and his colleagues "Scour the whole fucking house, turn the place over. I NEED some fucking evidence on this twat."

* * * * *

"Look I don't want to have to ask you this again Steven, where were you between the hours of 10 and 12 last night?"

"And I don't wanna fucking answer again."

Macca's lawyer whispered in his ear.

"Ok for the last time, I had a headache, I went to bed early."

"And can anybody vouch for this?"

"I live alone, so no."

"Let me put it to you this way then."

"Right this should be a laugh."

"At approximately 11:15 you were in the vicinity of Roberts Street and you saw a young lady walking alone, as she walked into Grant Thorold Park, you seized your opportunity and forcibly subjected her to a sexual assault."

"Oh right so you've got proof of that have you? My cum on her?"

"You know I haven't Steven because you know you wore a condom."

"I know fuck all mate, all I know is that I've got six sisters and you best catch this pervert before he touches one of them or we'll be in here talking about a murder."

"Come on Steven, make it easier for yourself, I know it's you, you know it's you, just admit it and make everyone's life easier."

"I'm telling you straight, you say it's me one more time and I'll knock you clean the fuck out. All you've got on me is some nebby old cunt who saw me running, which I've not been able to do without seeing one of you lot. Maybe ask your officers who always seem to follow me where I was last night."

"The interview was brought to an end by Detective Morris at 10:31."

∆ ∆ ∆

Lucas shuffled nervously outside the interview room, he knew Morris was not a man to be crossed and he knew he wasn't going to be happy with what he had to tell him. The trepidation became worse when an angry looking Morris left the interview room.

"Sir."

"Give me some good news Hughes, this bastard is too smug for his own good."

"Sorry sir, nothing in his house at all. No balaclavas, all we got from his trainers was half of Cleethorpes beach in his running shoes, no porn, the guy doesn't own a computer and we didn't even find any condoms. None of the neighbours saw him going out and not even a hint of drugs to do him on either."

"For fucks sake. The CPS would fucking laugh at me if I brought them this. I'm going to have to let this smug fucker go aren't I?"

"I don't know sir."

"Of course you fucking don't, watch him like a bastard hawk."

Morris punched the wall hard, denting the plaster and chipping the paintwork as he walked off cursing before letting out the loudest of primal screams. Hearing this in the interview room Macca turned to his lawyer and smiled.

# 2003

# Chapter 22

Checking he was still alive in his now accustomed way Ben opened his eyes to survey the room. He wasn't sure how long he'd been living here as time had stood still yet flown in equal measures. Minutes merged into hours which themselves merged into days. Days, weeks, months, who knew? Just existing rather than living, the dreams of yesterday firmly lost in the past. Essentially now just a waking nightmare as his elongated suicide to an eventual and inevitable death panned out in small bite size segments whilst daydreaming of a love and a life left behind and what might have been.

This morning the squat's usual stench of weed, heroin and crack smoke had been replaced by an overwhelming aroma of human excrement. Placing his hands to his crotch to make sure he hadn't shit himself, a relieved Ben lifted his hand back up to his nose to smell his putrid bollock sweat. He needed a shower more than anything but the hostel was an expensive and unnecessary luxury when he had a safe-ish roof over his head and bigger and better things to spend any money he might come by on. Beginning to ache in his legs and covered in a clammy sweat he scanned the room to find the syringe marked "B" then checked his pockets and suddenly realised he was out of gear and would have to make his daily trip into the real world much earlier than normal and without the comfort of a warm hit coursing in his blood and brain. Stumbling through the array of burnt foil, bent spoons, candles and carefully avoiding the dirty syringes Ben was pleased to get outside to the mid-morning sun and a nostril full of London pollution instead of the shit.

Never quite learning the layout of the local area had become both a blessing and a curse as he would discover new things or places and new people which kept his mind active but inevitably he would be late or take far too long to get where he wanted to be. Today was a day when all Ben needed to do was to get to where he needed to be in double fast time and get his situation sorted.

“Morning Ben, you’re early today, how are you?” Lorraine the pharmacy assistant greeted him

“All the better for seeing you” Ben half smiled back, conscious not to show his missing teeth and thinking back to a day before his libido and teeth disappeared that he’d never have come out with such a cheesy line, and that even though she was in her mid 50s he probably would have liked to fire into Lorraine.

“It’s a locum today, won’t be long.”

“Where’s Mark?”

“On a training course.”

“Oh right.”

The pharmacist looked at Ben like something he’d just stood in as Ben took a seat. Mark, the usual guy would have joined in the morning conversation and at least treated him like a human, however this guy’s scowls told Ben today’s daily transaction was not going to be pleasant. Starting to feel more sweat building on his skin and his stomach churning Ben sat patiently for 10 minutes, Lorraine mouthing “Sorry” to him on several occasions.

"Mr. Evans" the snooty pharmacist that Ben had taken a big dislike to called him forward to a shop now half-full of people waiting for their prescriptions.

"Yup that's me."

"Can I check the address please?"

"No Fixed Abode."

"Do you have any ID?"

"You tend not to have any when you don't have a house mate."

"I can't give you your methadone without any ID it's a controlled drug."

"Mate, look, I'm not being funny but I've been coming in months, the girls all know me and Mark usually takes me in the consult room to do this."

"Do you want your medicine or not?"

"I need my medicine mate!"

"Well do you have any ID?"

"No mate sorry, please? Lorraine?"

Lorraine took the pharmacist in the dispensary and came back a few moments later ushering Ben into the consultation room. Apologising profusely and then handing over his daily dose of sixty millilitres of sticky, sickly fluorescent green liquid Ben downed it in one and said goodbye. Fuming but not wanting to cause a scene he left the pharmacy and walked round the corner where he made himself sick into his water bottle capturing most of the methadone and a little bit of stomach bile.

"Fuck it" he thought remembering he should have picked his diazepam tablets up today as well. Concealing his bottle of bile infused opiate he made an about turn and back into the shop knowing full well he'd be in for another long wait and delighted in watching the locum squirm as he made the deliberate sneer of calling him a chemist and not a pharmacist.

With 30mg of his alleged daily intake of 10mg diazepam now in his stomach Ben made his way across South East London to see French and procure some of his and the capital's finest, heavily adulterated heroin. French was actually from the Democratic Republic of Congo and made his honest living in London under the guise of a French and Kikongo translator working in the embassy. At his understated bedsit Ben requested his usual weekly supply.

"I am sorry Mister Benjamin but you are well over your credit limit." French said in his usual drawl, somewhere in the middle of friendly and angry but not quite at either end of the spectrum "and this shit you try sell me, you think I am *dikaku,* I am *nkima,* I am stupid monkey yes?"

"No French mate. Come on it's got to be worth something?"

"Fifty mills of *kudia,* sorry stomach liquid and eleven *bule* diazepam. I give you one hit but you no take it in my house and you still owe lots of money Mister Benjamin and I not happy one bit, oh and no more crappy guitars to sell, I need cold hard cash monies, or passports."

"What should I do?"

"Get out there and pick pockets Mister Benjamin."

"Like a modern day Fagin you French."

"What you mean?"

"Forget it, can I have my gear?"

French passed Ben a small bag containing one measly shot of heroin and dismissed him with aplomb. With no needles upon his person and a withdrawal rattle developing, Ben's next stop was to find a pharmacy with the welcoming green and red arrows so he could pick up some clean works and get this hit in him to give him chance to function and take stock of how much French had just told him he owed. French always seemed relaxed when talking about money but Ben had heard the stories and didn't fancy a meeting with some machete wielding Congolese friends.

Wandering the streets almost aimlessly yet with severe purpose, his stomach cramping and the muscles in his legs jerking, Ben became distracted by two very pretty Scandinavian looking tourist girls who were obviously lost. Turning the charm up to maximum and using a skill set not seen since he frequented the pubs and clubs of North East Lincolnshire, Ben sold sand to the Arabs as he worked his magic on the two giggling girls. Moments later they had directions in completely the opposite direction of where they needed to be and he had a purse, a Danish passport and a mobile phone in his pockets plus an arrangement to meet both of them later for a drink and potential threesome that he would never show up for.

Finally Ben made it to a pharmacy and acquired some needles, spoons and the citric acid needed to make his hit soluble. Finding a quiet backstreet he cooked up half a shot, found a vein in his arm and released himself into his normality of escapism. Turning around Ben realised he was being watched by a tall man in a very expensive looking Hugo Boss suit who looked too well to do to be a copper and Ben assumed he was a banker or a trader who'd ventured out of the City for some reason or another, probably coke looking at him Ben thought.

"Alright mate? You lost?"

"No my friend I am not. I just wondered if a fine looking young man would like to earn himself a bit of extra money?"

"I always need extra money mate, what do I need to do?"

The man in the sharp suit undid his fly and pulled out a limp circumcised cock.

"How does £50 sound?"

Ben hesitated, he'd never even had thoughts about other men before and here he was face to face with not only a cock but the opportunity to make some much needed money.

"Err OK mate but I might not be very good. Never done it before."

"No problems."

Ben swallowed before mustering up as much spit as his heroin ravaged body would allow, taking the man's limp cock all the way into his mouth and beginning to suck. Hiding the taste of stale piss and unwashed bell end to the back of his mind as he felt the guy begin to stiffen. Remembering back to happier times when he used to get his sucked regularly and thinking about what he enjoyed, he lifted his hands up to start teasing the guys balls and shaft, working away til he was fully erect. Teasing his bell end with his tongue as he wanked him.

"Mmmmm you sure you've never done this before? You're a natural."

Sucking away as if his life depended on it, Ben took the guy as deep as his gag reflex would allow, all the time working on his shaft with his hands. Soon the cock began to tighten and pumped three big loads of hot salty cum down Ben's throat.

"Dirty smackhead faggot!"

A fist hit Ben's left temple, knocking him to the ground followed by a brogued foot straight into the bridge of his nose causing it to explode like a crimson blood firework, and then another foot into his mouth knocking out one of his remaining teeth. Ben spat out the tooth along with a mixture of blood and semen as the situation dawned on him.

"That wasn't worth 50 pence you dirty little faggot," as yet another shoe landed on his stomach forcing him to retch. The man turned away leaving Ben in a bloody mess on the floor. Ben saw red, a mist descended on his vision that he had not had since his days at the football as he got to his feet and ran full force at the man's back catching the back of his head with a mightily impressive right hand. The guy stumbled forward as Ben followed it up with several more right hands catching each one on the back of his head as he fell.

"I'm the fucking faggot am I? Im fucking Grimsby you cunt" Ben screamed as he rained more punches into the man's face fracturing his jaw and knocking him unconscious. Searching his pockets Ben liberated his wallet and then his expensive looking Tag Heuer. For good measure Ben stole his shoes too, just in case they were his or French's size as they looked quality.

Δ Δ Δ

The woman at the coffee shop was clearly uncomfortable serving a scruffy looking Ben with an obviously very recently broken nose, however she couldn't argue when he stated his money was just as good as everyone else's. Sat with his coffee Ben surveyed today's wage. One Danish passport, one expensive watch, one mobile phone, a pair of leather brogues and over a grand in cash, mainly £50 notes from the wanker banker but who cares? Money is money and French would probably accept US Dollars at a poor exchange rate as long as he was getting paid. Feeling the withdrawal starting again and aching from his earlier fracas, Ben contemplated banging up the remaining half hit in the coffee shop toilet but decided the woman was already watching him considerably and he wanted a full, decent size hit after today's escapades. Finishing his coffee, Ben got his bearings and headed, in the wrong direction at first, back to French's to pay off his debts and purchase his week's supply.

Back at the squat with the majority of his gear concealed, Ben began cooking up a big shot. Not too much to overdose but more than usual, he did after all deserve it after the day he'd had. Using his belt as a tourniquet he found his one remaining vein on his left arm, pierced the skin with the needle, drew back some blood then paused. Thinking of her long strawberry blonde hair a tear ran down Ben's cheek as he depressed the plunger and journeyed into another world.

# Chapter 23

Firing up the fryer for the evening shift, Stu cursed that he was missing a Monday night at home with a couple of cans. It wasn't his sister's fault she was poorly and Dad couldn't cope with the shop on his own since the breakdown but still. He'd tried to persuade them to sell the chippy but it had been in the family for generations and had a reputation as one of the best around - with fresh fish straight from the docks and his Grandad's family secret batter recipe. He'd agreed they should keep the shop but only if he didn't have to work too much there. Now it was becoming more frequent and he thought they were taking the piss a little bit. Mixing his Grandad's batter for tonight's customers he thought he would kind of missed this place if they had have sold it. The majority of his childhood memories revolved around the family chippy and he'd made good friends sitting chatting over a bag of scraps. Moving on to the potatoes and chipping machine he laughed as he realised he actually quite enjoyed it despite his protestations.

He looked at the clock as Darren knocked on the door, 20 minutes til opening which meant he was 10 minutes late. He should really give him a bollocking but he didn't like acting like the boss and besides he saw Darren more as a mate. Even though he was much younger, he could have a laugh with him and Darren was into the same sort of music and they'd had many pissed conversations on the Riverhead.

"Alright Daz?"

"Alright Stu. Soz I'm late mate."

"Don't worry mate, can you sort out the peas for us?"

Turning up the CD when a tune they both liked came on the boys chatted about music and girls from up Gullivers they had either shagged or wanted to shag until they opened up, carrying on the conversation in between customers with a variety of positions and scenarios involved, including the weeping willow tree on the way out towards the Heratige Centre and Sainsbury's.

A group of girls Darren knew from college came in and flirted with Stu til he gave in and gave them free chips in exchange for the brunette's number. He'd text her later and try get her to go to Gullies with him at the weekend. Maybe try out Darren's up against the tree suggestion at the willow.

Frying a fresh order of haddock for the next customers Darren swore loudly as some of the fat splashed back on his hand

"Fuck that's hot!"
"It'll only be the temperature."
"Fuck off!"

Helping Darren out and running his hand under cold water Stu kept asking Darren more questions about the brunette who, it turned out was quite into him.

They then went quiet until it was just before closing time, as Macca walked in scurrying in his wallet and ordering a bag of chips with extra scraps.

"You want salt and vinegar on that mate?"

∆ ∆ ∆

Macca had been having a shit day at work, his boss really leaning into him and pushing his luck and then to top it off he'd just found out no one in his family had had the common decency to tell him about Hannah being poorly again. He fucking hated his family sometimes but loved them to bits too. He'd do anything to protect any of his sisters, especially Hannah the baby. Pissed off he decided to go round to his Mums to get the full story and maybe an explanation as to why they decided not to tell him. On his way there a car pulled up beside him.

"Evening Mr MacKenzie, going anywhere nice?"

It was that fucking pig Morris and his new bum chum Hughes. Why the fuck couldn't they just leave him alone? There'd not been a rape for at least a year and there was never enough proof to attach Macca to them in the first place. God he wish he could find out which nebby old biddy had grassed on him to the police.

"Just round to my Mums if that's alright with you or do I have to get fucking permission to walk anywhere nowadays?"

"Come on now Steven there's no need to be like that."

"Yes there fucking is, I can't take a shit without you being there."

"Mind your language please Steven or I'll have to arrest you."

"Again, haven't you got bored of that and letting me go?"

"I will get you, you know? One day you'll mess up and I'll be there waiting."

"I'm sure you will but I've told you a thousand times I'm not your man, now please just leave me alone, this is harassment this."

Morris drove off chuckling to himself and said to Hughes "one day he's gonna be careless I just know it."

Macca continued to his Mum's house where he wasn't in the mood for civilities, all he wanted to know was why he wasn't told. After a steaming argument, made more embarrassing by having to conceal his hard on, he'd stormed out the house. Why did that happen every time he got mad? It was worse than when he was a teenager and he couldn't stop getting hard ons looking at girl's bras at school.

Starving, but just about calm now, he stormed into the chippy just before it closed. He checked his wallet and could only muster up enough for a bag of chips.

"You want salt and vinegar on that mate?"

"Yeah."

"Open or wrapped?"

"Open and a fork."

Macca sat down on the shop's window ledge and ate his tea.

∆ ∆ ∆

"You know who that was don't you?" Daz asked like an excited schoolboy not realising Macca was still in the shop.

"Yeah Steven 'Macca' MacKenzie, why?"

"Well my mate reckons he's the number one suspect for the beast."

"Yeah I know he was arrested and questioned and that but I reckon it's a load of bollocks."

"Why's that then?"

"Well, haven't you ever heard the stories?" Stu obviously also oblivious to the sedentary Macca inside the shop.

"What stories?"

"Well, there was this one time he tried to fuck a barmaid from the Jube and couldn't get it up, serious mister floppy, then she found him having a wank watching a video/"

"Really?"

"Yeah and you'll never guess what the sick cunt was watching at the time?"

"No go on."

"You ever seen Scum?"

"Yeah, the snooker ball in the sock bit?"

"No mate, worse, the greenhouse bit."

"The rape?"

"Yeah dirty bastard!"

"So he likes rape, he could be the beast?"

"But that was gay rape wannit? I reckon he just gets off on violence. They reckon he's always hard when scrapping at the footy and apparently..." Stu made a sign with his little finger to indicate a small penis

"Fuck off, all that true?"

"Apparently so, I know lads who went to footy fights with him."

"Fuck me that's just weird. Hasn't he got like 4 sisters?"

"Six mate, all fit, I'd shag em all at the same time."

"Oh yeah?"

"Yeah especially the youngest one Hannah, great set of jugs."

"Isn't she a bit nuts?"

"Absolutely fucking barmy but I reckon that'd make her a real dirty fuck."

"CCCCUUUUUUNNNNNNNNNTTTTTT!!!"

Macca leapt over the counter and grabbed Stu's long hair through his hair net. Using the momentum from the jump he rammed his head into the wall, repeating several times until blood oozed out of Stu's forehead and erupted from his splattered nose.

"CUNT CUNT CUNT!"

Turning him around Macca kneed him in the bollocks three times before punching his non existent nose then grabbing his hair again, turning him around and pushing his head into the fryer. Stu's screams were momentarily drowned out by the sound of the bubbling fat and the repetition of Macca daring him to "fucking say it again" as he ducked his head up and down in the sizzling cauldron.

The air of the chip shop, usually a smell of fresh fish and vinegar, was tainted by the bacon like aroma of cooking flesh, burnt hair and the smells of Stu's urine and faeces, Darren's vomit and the fresh semen that Macca had just ejaculated into his boxer shorts.

Δ Δ Δ

“Grab your coat Hughes” Morris said with extreme enthusiasm and a beaming smile after putting down the phone “we’ve fucking got him bang to rights this time”

# Chapter 24

Tim watched the foam of bubbles move down the sloped sides of the latte glass as he considered the world. Sitting here in the coffee shop close to his central Manchester flat had become his daily routine since Ian had moved out to the Stockport suburbs with Rosie. Investing his money wisely he now had an impressive property portfolio and a rent income which eclipsed all of his peer's salaries and afforded him time to concentrate on his club nights without having to worry about the daily grind and the overall success of his latest project. This freedom had made the night's a huge success as it was obviously done for the love of the scene and music and thus the vibe of the night was mellow and not stained by the chasing of the filthy lucre.

"You want another one Tim?" Gina called over to him. Tim nodded. He really fancied Gina but liked her too much as a person and liked her coffee far too much to make things awkward by telling her so. Watching her round arse as she moved her not even 5 foot frame round the counter to grind his beans and warm his milk he fantasised about her curves in sexy underwear.

"New beans today, Ethiopian, Fair Trade, you like them?"

"Yeah, lovely" Tim lied - he couldn't taste any difference to normal - "You coming on Saturday Gina?" he asked talking about his next club night.

"Yeah I hope so, is Rosie and Jim gonna be there?"

"I don't know, Ian hasn't text me back yet."

As he foolishly motioned with his phone in case Gina didn't understand what he meant by texting a beep went off in his hand. As if he'd heard them talking about him it was Ian.

What's pink and smells of holly?

Tim rang Ian, tempted to say the punch line of the joke but deciding that Gina and her customers might be too polite company to hear him shout it out across her coffee shop.

"You sick sod."

"You've heard it then?"

"Yeah, the sick bastard went to our school, so did she, year above, my mate Ben made the beast with two backs with her."

"Fucking hell I hope you've taken the piss."

"Would have done mate, but he doesn't answer his phone anymore, he's gone off the radar. Anyway you and Rosie coming on Saturday."

"Shit, I'd forgotten all about it but yeah should be able to come, anyway I didn't text you just to tell you the joke, just read something about Grimsby in today's paper and I thought of you."

"Let me guess something to do with fish?"

"Well sort of it says 'man hunt for chippy attacker. Humberside police are on the lookout for a man who deep fried somebody's head in an unprovoked attack'"

"Fucking hell, first I've heard of it, I'll text our Karl and get the goss, see you Saturday then yeah?"

"Yes mate."

Hanging up just as Gina put his latte down he thanked her and retold the story to her as he sugared and stirred his drink.

"Oh god that's awful, the poor guy."

"I know! I'm gonna text my brother and find out what's happened" again wiggling his phone when saying text. Shaking his head internally Tim wished that, just for once, he could act normally around a girl he fancied.

Tapping out the text to Karl he was momentarily distracted as he noticed Gina's nice big round arse bent over the counter and very nearly messaged Karl what he would like to do to Gina. Quickly deleting the phrase "up the shitter" he sent the text.

Chip shop attack? What's the story?

Sipping his coffee while secretly watching Gina from a distance a text came back indicating it was Ben's mate Stu.

He's quiet as a mouse. You sure?

You daft cunt. It was him who got attacked. Macca done him

Cheers mate. BTW what's pink and smells of holly?

Seeing the words Macca brought back many memories for Tim. Not only that stolen summer with Hannah spending what was his only comfortable time in the presence of a girl he liked, albeit a very young one, but also of the awful ensuing vivid nightmares and panic attacks.

During his afternoon gym session images of Hannah kept visualising in Tim's head as he regretted his decisions not to keep in touch with her and hoped she was ok. Wondering what she was up to nowadays and did she hate him? He certainly deserved to be hated after what he had done to her but she was cool, young and pretty so he was certain she'd have found someone to love her like she wanted him to do and he now appreciated that he should have done. Walking home from the gym with thoughts still firmly on

Hannah he got to his flat and booted up the computer. Logging on to Friends Reunited he saw no sign of Hannah but her best mate Gemma, the slag, was on there. Reasoning that they were so close back then that they must still be in touch he sent her a quick message.

Hi Gemma,

Not sure if you remember me, I'm Tim, Karl White's brother. How you doing nowadays?

He thought about asking after Hannah but didn't want to seem too obvious that was his only reason for messaging her, plus Hannah was bound to have told her about him so he was certain the message would have got to her. So he simply signed off

Get Back

Tim x

Going out on to the balcony for a fag Tim looked out over the canals of Manchester and pondered all the people he'd left behind in Grimsby and wondered what they were all up to. Karl was studying Law at Lincoln uni commuting every day - he smiled at the irony of such a little scrote like Karl who spent most of his teenage years in other people's cars evading the law had now chosen to dedicate his life to the legal profession.

Mum and Ray seemed to be doing OK on the few times he'd remembered to phone them, his Dad was still being his Dad - propping up the bar at the Jube and moaning about what they'd done to the place after the rebuild.

Last he'd heard of Ben he was in London chasing the dream with his music and had a girlfriend and as for everyone else, he didn't have a clue what they were doing, nor did he particularly care one way or the other. He did now know that Macca was on the run from the old bill after deep frying someone's face - sick bastard. At least if Gemma got back in touch he might find out about Hannah and get some gossip on everyone else. Back inside he made some calls about Saturday night's event then had a wank thinking about a hybrid of a young Hannah and Gina before showering and retiring to bed with his book.

The next morning Tim checked his emails before going for his morning walk, coffee and flirting session with Gina. There was a message from Gemma.

Hi Tim,

Of course I remember you! How could I forget?! How are you? I heard you were a big shot music promoter in Manchester nowadays. I'm across there this weekend if you can suggest a decent night out.

I'm stuck in Gy doing agency work at Youngs, pays shit and I stink of fish most the time but I'm happy I suppose.

Anyway I'd love to chat and maybe see you at the weekend? I promise most of me won't smell like haddock. Here's my number hit me up

Saving her number in his phone Tim text Gemma to make sure he had the right number and promised to ring her later. Wondering why she hadn't mentioned Hannah he began to be a little upset that maybe he didn't mean that much to her but also relieved that he hadn't hurt her too much. Arriving at the busier than usual coffee shop Gina started to make his latte before he'd even ordered while he stood blatantly staring at her curves. Taking a seat he pondered his current and former lives and realised that the one thing missing in both was love. He hadn't had a date for months and although he was comfortable talking to girls he never felt brave enough to actually ask them out.

A few coffees and a good few stares at Gina's arse later Tim made his way home and decided to ring Gemma.

"Hey stranger" She answered straight away, almost too friendly considering they were, at best, passing acquaintances

"Hey how are you?"

"Yeah, I'm good, fed up and tired from work but I've got this weekend to look forward to. You gonna tell me where to meet you?"

"Ha ha well yeah, I'm err putting a night on so suppose I could sneak you and your mates on the guest list if you fancy it?"

"Sounds good, I'll be wearing my new dress, think you'll like it. Plenty of thigh and cleavage on show"

Tim felt a twinge in his pants as his cock grew semi hard thinking about Gemma in her dress and that she was blatantly flirting with him.

"Sounds nice, I'm sure I won't be the only one admiring it."

"Yes but if you're a good boy, you'll be the only one seeing what's underneath"

"Oh really?"

"Only if you're very good."

"So who you coming over with?" Tim asked changing the subject slightly and hoping to get Hannah into the conversation.

"Oh some girls from work."

"Anyone I'd know? Anyone from school?"

"No I'm not really in touch with anyone I used to hang around with"

Bollocks thought Tim, he bit the bullet.

"Not even Hannah MacKenzie? You two were practically joined at the hip weren't you?"

"Yeah, still friends but she's not coming, she's not been well, she's in errr....... hospital at the moment."

"Oh right, nothing too serious I hope?"

"Well erm.......I'm not sure I should say."

"Please."

"Well ok, erm.... she's in the psychiatric ward."

"Bloody hell I never knew she had problems, is she ok?"

"Well yeah it all started in year 9 when she started to cut herself because of some older guy she had been seeing over summer. I was meant to be her best friend, and I didn't even know she was seeing anyone. Well anyway he basically abandoned her, and she started cutting, stubbing fags on her arms and legs, you know?"

"Oh right. Did she say who?" Tim began to worry

"No but if I ever find out, he's dead meat."

"Yeah, I'm sure" Tim's worries were relieved and heightened in equal measures

"So anyway she's carried on hurting herself all through school, none of us knew, I'd have helped if I had."

"Of course you would."

"So anyway she tried to top herself when Steven, err Macca, was first arrested about the beast stuff. Took a load of tablets, and anyway, we all thought she was ok, you know better because of the medication until about six weeks ago she starts talking about seeing ghosts."

"Ok. What sort of ghosts?"

"Only the baby she had aborted in year 11, I didn't even know about that either, she wouldn't tell me who the dad was just that it was complicated and linked to the other guy in some way."

What the fuck? Thought Tim. Karl and Hannah?

"So she doesn't know about the chippy thing then?"

"God news travels! And no. Nobody dare tell her."

"Fuck."

"Yeah I know."

Tim changed the subject matter to other things as quickly as he could without giving too much away.

"God have you seen the time?" Gemma eventually said.

"Oh yeah, best let you go. See you Saturday then?"

"Oh yes you will. I've wanted to fuck you for a long time."

"We'll see."

"Oh no we won't! It's a date."

Tim hung up, mind racing between thoughts of him making Hannah so poorly she was cutting herself, Karl getting Hannah pregnant and him fucking Gemma on Saturday night.

He woke up to a message from Gemma.

Hey sexy thinking bout your cock on Saturday G xx

He replied with his standard response to anything a little risqué

Oh really? X

Then made his way out for his coffee where Gina was looking better than he had ever seen her before. As she made his latte she caught him looking at her arse and gave it a wiggle. Tim was flustered when she gave him his drink and even more so when she came over.

"Tim, you've been looking for months, when are you gonna ask me out?"

"Erm......"

"Tell you what I'll let you buy me a drink on Saturday, how does that sound?"

"Great Gina."

"Great. It's a date then."

Δ Δ Δ

The phone reception in the club was, as always, absolutely shocking and the only places to get bars of signal were either right next to the speaker stack or at the entrance and neither were particularly conducive to being able to make the call Tim needed to. The main DJ for his night hadn't shown yet and was due on in twenty minutes. Fearing that people would kick off if he didn't show Tim was frantically pacing up and down beside the bouncers trying to connect the call whilst appeasing the revellers with his usual charm. On the plus side, it seemed that Gemma had forgotten all about her slaggy promise to him and was also nowhere to be seen and Gina was looking stunning tonight despite her plate sized dilated pupils and gurning lips that the ecstasy had given her. Tim had found himself a little jealous of some guys she'd been kissing and hugging before he'd realised she was pilling - the green-eyed monster dissipating as soon as he realised and it was his turn. He'd slipped her the tongue as they kissed and she'd reciprocated.

Tim was relieved as the call connected - "sorry mate got stuck in traffic on the M6, I'm literally parking up now" only to be equally as disheartened to hear a Grimsby accent - "I'm on the fucking VIP list I'm a mate of Tim's" as he turned to see Gemma's wave of brown curls arguing with the bouncer on the door, clearly over-inebriated on booze. As he darts over to stop this escalating into any trouble the overpowering smell of Clinique Happy mixed with orange Bacardi Breezer comes off Gemma. Placing an arm round the bouncer's huge shoulders he placates him and ushers the walking STD to the roped off area.

"Can I get you a drink?" He says motioning to the young waitress as he departs to work the room leaving Gemma alone to drink herself into a stupor.

The room fills with excitement as the music stops and lights go dark. One solitary green laser beam sweeps across the dance floor, shapes lighting up eager faces as the crowd clap in unison. A spotlight hits the DJ booth to show the main act in a sombrero as everyone cheers expecting him to drop his summer hit from last year.

"Don't stop moving to the S Club beat."

The crowd look at each other bemused, the bewilderment is almost tangible before a hard house bass line and kick drum take over mixed with tracks from S Club 7, Blue and 5ive as the DJ laughs uncontrollably. The music slows and the lights flicker and Tim thinks there has been a power surge before the DJ ramps it back up in another mirth filled game with the ecstasy and amphetamine fuelled crowd. The DJ is clearly in a playful mood as he toys with the dancers casually dropping Madchester anthems in behind Balearic beats. As he walks amongst the dance floor Tim is praised for another successful night as he finds Gina who throws her arms around him singing The Stone Roses.

"Sometimes I fantasise" she screams in his face before planting a tender, yet impassioned, kiss on his lips. Through his one open eye Tim spies an extremely irate Gemma attempt to stand up as her heel buckles underneath her. The crowd near her cheer as she is escorted to the exit by the bouncers screaming obscenities at anyone who'll listen and pointing at Tim dropping the C word exceptionally violently.

# Chapter 25

Vikki sobbed into Suzi's shoulder as the hearse carrying her Dad's coffin pulled up at what was now her house in New Waltham. With her Mum and Dad now both gone and being an only child she was now glad of the bond her and Suzi had even if they hadn't been so close in recent times. She'd warned her Dad about smoking and eating too much red meat but he'd always laughed and said he'd be ok. The massive heart attack he'd had in his sleep saw to the fact he wasn't ok and Vikki cried more thinking about how she wasn't there for him when he went, too busy following her own dream career as a nurse in London. Not that she was living much of a dream since Ben had disappeared without a trace nor an explanation. She must have done something wrong, had she come on too strong? He was the one who said he loved her first, she'd just continued it. Maybe she had fallen in love too quickly and should have realised when he was wearing his socks in bed that something wasn't quite right. Ben was gone, her Mum was gone, her Dad now gone, she was alone other than Suzi and Auntie Jackie. Thank God for them.

They got in the big blue funeral car and drove down Peakes Parkway towards the crematorium. Dad had never been religious other than singing "Abide with me" when the cup final was on the telly so she'd decided for just a simple service at the crem. They walked into the packed room and Vikki felt relief that so many people thought enough of her Dad to turn out for him, the nagging doubt of them only being there for a piss up and free sandwiches had long gone. She scanned the room secretly hoping to see Ben, but all she saw were sympathetic smiles. She'd give anything for a big hug with Ben right now, fact she'd give anything just to see his smile. A rush of guilt came over her as she realised she should be thinking about giving anything just to see her Dad's smile once more and that set her sobs off causing her to be sick in her mouth. The acid burnt as she swallowed it back down and cried more, snot and tears streaming down her face smudging her make up.

Δ Δ Δ

As she got out of the car at the Harvest Moon all Vikki wanted to do was go back to her Dad's house and curl up in a ball, she certainly didn't need a woman she didn't know from Adam telling her how pretty she was and that her Dad would be proud of her, especially when her singledom and this woman's grandson started being brought into the conversation. Making her excuses, Vikki abruptly left and entered the pub, barging past all the sympathetic faces to the toilet. Looking at her puffy eyes and smudged make up in the mirror Vikki laughed then cried as Suzi walked in looking for her.

"Waterproof mascara bollocks, I look like a fucking panda."

"No you don't, you're beautiful as always. I only came in to make sure you was ok and did you want red or white?"

"Red please, Shiraz if they've got it, a fucking large one. I'll be out in a minute I just need to sort my daft self out."

Vikki washed her face and reapplied her make up before having a wee then preparing herself for going out to face the other mourners.

She sat with Suzi and Suzi was a rock for her, batting off sleazy drunk old men and changing the conversation rapidly whenever an elderly distant relative questioned her about being single and starting a family alongside keeping her glass of wine topped up.

"Come on" said Suzi "let's go outside for a bit"

Vikki stood up and realised she was a bit tipsy. She'd not eaten properly for days and the adrenaline comedown after the funeral coupled with several large glasses of Shiraz had taken its toll. She walked linking arms with Suzi until they got outside.

"Give us one of them Suze" she said as Suzi took a fag out of the golden Benson & Hedges packet.

"You've given up"
"I know, but if I can't have one today when can I have one?"

"It was a valid point and Suzi offered the packet to Vikki before cupping her hand around the lighter to give her fire. Vikki took a deep inhale followed by a spluttering cough.

"Jesus they taste shit but I've sure missed them."

Suzi laughed. Vikki was coping surprisingly well with today all things considered.

"You know they're all talking about me being single?"

"Yeah, ignore them, do what you want to do."

"Well the thing is there kinda is, err.... was somebody."

"Oh right."

The girls paused for what seemed an eternity as one of the elderly Aunts opened the door to outside thinking it was the toilet. Laughing Suzi said

"So you gonna tell me about him or what?"

"I can't, it's complicated."

"So it's a her?"

"Oh God no! He's definitely all man."

"So why can't you tell me?"

"Well you know Ben who was up Gullies on your hen do?"

"Oh him, I tried to warn you he was trouble. Proper ladies man and knows it."

"Well I met him, by accident, in a pub in London."

"Wow you saw him twice that's more than I got."

"What?!"

"Oh come on Vikki most of Grimsby has had his big dick, you must know that, carry on."

"So actually, I saw him a lot more than twice."

"You tamed the beast, well done."

Vikki started to blub. Suzi held her tight.

"Oh, come on, I'm sorry it was a joke, so you were serious about him?"

"Yeah, we saw each other every day, we was going out, proper boyfriend and girlfriend for months, he said he loved me."

"What happened?"

"He disappeared."

"What you mean he disappeared?"

“Exactly what I say, he’d started to go a bit odd with people, me, my friends, his own friends, then.” Vikki started to cry again.

“Then uh then he vanished.”

“People don’t just vanish Vik.”

“He fucking did, stopped paying rent, stopped turning up to work, stopped living at where he was living. One of my old flat mates reckons she saw him begging, so I went to where she said but no. Just gone. I fucking loved him Suze, and I thought he loved me. Then he left me, just like Mum left me, just like Dad’s gone now.”

The tears exploded from Vikki’s eyes as she took a turn for the worse, Suzi holding her tight and stroking her strawberry blonde locks. Patting her comfortingly whilst finishing her fag and wishing she’d brought her drink out.

“Ben is a fucking cunt but I still fucking love him” she heard Vikki mutter through the tears as she held her.

"Come on darl lets get you another drink."

"Can we get fucking leathered Suze?"

"Let's wait for the oldies to go home then yeah we can."

∆ ∆ ∆

Coming back with two tequilas each Vikki was well on her way to achieving her goal. She made sure she gave an extra lean forward at the bar when she noticed a group of teenage lads checking out her arse in her tight black dress and heels. Suzi noticed and pulled her up on it and she proclaimed it was just a bit of harmless fun and what's wrong with teasing now and then?

Several rounds later the pub had run out of tequila and the girls now necked Baileys as if it were milk. Sharing Suzi's last cigarette a practically incoherent Vikki slurred as she told once again of how she was alone and she missed her Dad and she missed Ben, the love of her life. Suzi, not feeling the effects of the alcohol as much as her cousin, was a little exasperated and sought solace by going to the toilet alone. After 5 minutes of peace with her own thoughts she returned to find Vikki talking to the table of young men.

"Which one of you is gonna come and give me the fuck of my life?"

"Victoria!! Sorry guys she's a bit drunk it was her Dad's funeral today."

"And now I'm all alone but one of these hunks is going to keep me company tonight."

"Oh no they're not, come on let's get you home."

Linking arms and practically forcing her away from the table Suzi persuaded Vikki to leave the pub and head back to her Dad's house. On the way, elongated by Vikki's staggering, Vikki grabbed a handful of her red hair.

"I'm little orphan Annie" she said before erupting in a fit of laughter which soon descended into another bout of sobbing.

"Come on let's get you back to your house."

"It's my fucking Dad's house."

"It's yours now darl."

More tears.

∆ ∆ ∆

Her head was banging as though workmen had a pneumatic drill on her temple and it felt like a thousand badgers had taken a shit in her mouth. Vikki, still in her dress and heels, opened her puffy eyes to find herself on the sofa. The singing and other noises from the kitchen indicated that Suzi had stayed the night and was making breakfast. As Vikki took her shoes off Suzi entered the front room carrying a tray.

"Morning princess" she cheerily said as the smell of toast wafted into Vikki's nose causing her stomach to flip and her mouth fill with saliva. Vikki ran to the toilet just making it in time before last night's heady mix of wine, tequila and Baileys escaped violently from her mouth and nostrils. Washing her face and going to the bedroom to put on some more comfortable and appropriate attire Vikki returned to the front room to Suzi sat down finishing the remaining toast and reading last night's Evening Telegraph.

"Sorry about that, and sorry if I did anything bad last night, I honestly can't remember a thing."

"Oh it's fine babe, as long as you're ok."

"I'm fine except feeling rougher than a badger's arse."

"That's ok then."

"Thanks for staying."

"It's ok, I text John early to let him know I wouldn't be home."

"Thanks Suze, you're a darl."

"It's ok darl."

Vikki laid back down on the sofa as Suzi returned to the Evening Telegraph.

"What's happening in Gy then?"

"Oh the main bits all about that lad who deep fried half of someone's face, he got sent down yesterday."

"I heard about that, fucking horrible."

"Yeah, this town gets worse every day."

"I miss it though."

"You're mad."

Suzi shook her head and continued reading while Vikki dozed.

"Hey Vik, this'll interest you 'shortage of nurses at Princess Diana Hospital' you should apply."

"You know what, I might just do that"

"Seriously?"

"Yeah why not?, I've got nothing in London and I've already got a house here."

# 2008

# Chapter 26

Macca had been woken up again. He scanned around the small room. HMP Manchester, Strangeways, B Wing. His home for the past two and a bit years since they'd transferred him from Lincoln with no explanation. His pad mate Wes snoring his head off as always. The wonderful solution that the screws in healthcare had come up with for Wes's snoring was for Wes to wear a plaster across his nose like a modern day Robbie Fowler and for Macca to wear foam earplugs. Neither of these things had helped one single bit, and it was driving Macca nuts.

Some of the more scientific minded (or indeed desperate) inmates had figured out a way to make a hooch using Fortisip nutritional drinks and vitamin B tablets, fermenting them on the radiator. They had drunk some last night to celebrate his release but even the buzz from the vomit flavoured alcohol disguised with orange juice couldn't help him drift off. If anything it was making matters worse - exacerbating Wes' snoring and causing a surge of Macca's stomach acid making his heartburn worse than ever.

There was a number of things Macca was looking forward to on the outside. The first was some proper Gaviscon liquid for his painful heartburn rather than the foamy tablets he had to have in here. Apparently the glass bottle could be used as a weapon so he couldn't have the liquid while on the inside. He also couldn't wait to see the back of those horrendous green jogging bottoms. Not only were they scratchy but they were an insult to his eyes too, unflattering and a colour that made you wish you were blind. The fashion police should have whoever decided on those in here for life, but on E Wing with the beasts so nobody could get to them. But most of all, most of all he couldn't wait to have a decent night's kip in a comfortable bed without Wes's jet engine adenoids rattling the walls of the room. That would be tonight he thought to himself as he tried to block the snoring out and drift off back to sleep without battering Wes and buying himself yet more time at Her Majesty's pleasure.

∆ ∆ ∆

"Last day today MacKenzie?"

"Yes Miss" Macca replied engaging in conversation after confirming his name and number.

"And we're not going to see you again soon are we?"

"No Miss, gonna find myself a nice girl like you and live my life properly."

Macca had built up quite a rapport with Cardwell during his stay in Manchester's premier category A hotel. Amanda, although Macca shouldn't really have known her real name, was a thick set, masculine looking woman from Ashton Under Lyne with short, yet feminine, brown hair that Macca had developed more than a little crush for. So much so it had become that blatantly obvious that Wes and all the other inmates took the piss almost constantly. Yes he knew nothing could happen with him being a con and her being a screw, and yes he knew she was in a relationship. And yes, he even knew she was a lesbian so she wouldn't be interested at all but she was the only non-relative female he'd ever actually been able to talk to without clamming up or being embarrassed, so he wasn't kidding when he said a girl like her.

"So we'll take you to reception and then transport will take you back to Lincoln ready for letting you out to your family. That sound good?"

"Yes Miss, I can't wait."

"Stay out of trouble MacKenzie," she whispered "I like you but I never want to see you again."

"Yes Miss."

Δ Δ Δ

Walking down the hill to reception, high barbed wire fencing to his left, Macca looked over his right shoulder to the imposing tower in the middle of Strangeways hoping that it would be the last time he ever saw the inside of this place, or indeed any place like this. After being processed he was led to the van that would take him, unnecessarily in his eyes, to Lincoln and on his way to being a free man. The tyres rattled loudly on the motorway floor, a gentle soothing loud hum that calmed Macca into a very deep sleep.

"MacKenzie!" Shouted the guard "MacKenzie!"

Macca woke up, the guard shaking him awake as they arrived at HM Prison Lincoln. Going through the seemingly pointless reception that all new prisoners undertook to be led to the door and released into society.

Macca closed his eyes and took a deep breath, somewhat surprised that the air of a free man smelt exactly the same as one of a man who was incarcerated. Opening his eyes his crying Mum was running towards him, nearly knocking him over with the force of the hug she gave him. His mother stood back and looked him up and down

"There's nothing on you, didn't those bastards feed you?"

Only bread and water Mam."

“As it should be! Well, anyway, we’ve booked a table at Damon’s before we drive back, I’m gonna treat my baby to an onion loaf.”

The thought of a Damon’s burger made Macca’s mouth water, but he was also anxious about being in public, particularly as he felt that in his clothes which were fashionable 5 years ago that he had the look and smell of prison on him, but he couldn’t upset his Mum and she wouldn’t have let him win the argument anyway, not today.

In the front passenger seat of the car with Jodie driving and Mum and Clare in the back, the welcome party section of the MacKenzie clan drove the short distance from the prison to the restaurant. As the funny roof of the round building came into view, a knot hit Macca’s stomach as his heart started to race and his chest felt like it would explode. His lungs burnt as his throat closed up and he gasped for air, salty tears building in his eyes as the oxygen left his body and a tourniquet tightened strongly around his chest.

“Steven? Steven are you ok?” Jodie shook his knee

"I........can't.........fuck........ing..........breathe."

"Look at him, Jodie stop the car for fuck's sake." screamed Mum

"Oh my god he's fucking dying." cried Clare

"I'm..........fine.........calm.........down."

"Clare calm the fuck down." shouted Mum "Jodie he needs a paper bag, it's just like our Hannah."

"What he's fucking nuts?" Asked Jodie

"Shut up!" Said Mum swinging but missing a slap in Jodie's direction

"Help..........me............help" cried Macca now in inconsolable blubs.

"Jodie I won't ask again, stop the fucking car!"

Jodie pulled over, Mum got out and in a manner she'd become far too accustomed to when dealing with her youngest offspring she eventually helped calm Macca's hyperventilating by means of a paper bag and calm talking. They sat in silence for ten minutes.

"Can we get our fucking burger now? I'm starving." moaned Jodie.

“It’s up to Steven,” replied Mum “and I never brought you up to be such an inconsiderate cow! Steven what do you want to do.”

“Let’s eat, I want that onion loaf you promised.”

*****

Jodie had been laughing to herself occasionally on the drive home but it took until Caistor until Clare eventually asked

“What the bloody hell you laughing at?”

“Our Ste.”

“What about me?”

“I’m dying I’m dying help me.”

“Fuck off!”

“Jodie behave, Steven mind your language!” Mum piped up from the back

“And did you see how you clammed up when the waitress spoke to you? I know she was pretty but bloody hell! Err.... err..... burger and onion loaf please.” she said mockingly

“Fuck off!” Macca raised his voice, clearly irate

"And I know it's been 5 years since you had straight sex."

"What the fucks that supposed to mean?"

"Well you know, all guys together."

"What the fuck you trying to say?"

"I bet you were the first dropping the soap in the shower."

"FUCK OFF!!"

Steve landed a hard punch on Jodie's thigh that caused her to swerve the car and made her whole leg go dead. It also caused an embarrassing erection as strong as the steel holding up the Humber Bridge in Macca's pants.

"I'm not a fucking queer" he said shuffling in his seat so his Mum and sisters couldn't see his hard on. Mum reprimanding everybody, even Clare who had been silent throughout the whole situation. The rest of the journey was spent in an uncomfortable hush as nobody dare say any more, scared of upsetting Steven or Mum.

Turning onto the street where they'd all grown up Mum told Macca she'd made up his old bedroom and he was welcome to stay there until he got back on his feet and could afford his own place. Entering the front room Hannah had adorned it in balloons and let off a party popper before running over and giving Macca a big bear hug.

"God I've missed you Steven."
"Missed you too Hannah, you're looking well."
"I'm feeling it at the minute."
"Good."

Catching up with all the local news and gossip with his family until the early hours of the morning Macca eventually retired to his old room. The bed was far too soft as he tossed and turned trying to get to sleep. The house was eerily quiet, too quiet and the lack of earplugs felt weird. Exhausted and tired but unable to get to sleep Macca tugged and pulled hard at his bell end hoping for an erection that was nowhere close to developing nor never would. His heartburn sizzled in his chest so he got up and swigged a gulp out of the Gaviscon bottle. Laying back in the far too comfortable bed he tried again to wank himself to sleep but once again no matter how much painful pulling and tugging occurred not even the slightest drop of blood entered his cavernous tissue and there was no signs of any developing stiffness.

"Fuck it I'm off for a run."

# Chapter 27

BEEP BEEP BEEP BEEP

Kerry hit the snooze button on her alarm clock once again knowing full well this was the fourth time and she really was going to be late for her shift if she didn't get a move on, but her bed was warm and it was dark and miserable outside. Who in their right mind started work at 6 o'clock in the morning? At least it was money, albeit poor, she thought as she fought off the doziness and tried to ready herself, and at least she didn't have to worry about looking good in a shower cap cum hair net combo she convinced herself as she scraped her greasy blonde hair back into a high ponytail. She really should have had a shower and washed her hair last night she thought as she caught a sniff of fish from yesterday's shift on the fillet separator coupled with stale sweat. Fuck it, she thought, everyone who worked at Youngs stank of fish, nobody would notice. For fuck's sake nearly everyone in Grimsby smelt of fish from the factories.

Pulling on yesterday's bra, ill-fitting and grey from being washed with darks, and a pair of pants she looked at her semi naked self in the mirror and thought "you fucking meff" and said out loud "no wonder you haven't got a fella" as she grabbed some jogging bottoms and a jumper and set off for today's 8 hour slog separating frozen fish fillets into different sizes and sending them off to the other parts of the factory for further processing. Oh how she dreamt of her former glory days and glamour of the Bird's Eye fish finger line.

Stepping out into the drizzle for the long walk down Cromwell Road a bleary eyed Kerry was nearly knocked over by a guy running.

"You could have said fucking sorry!" She shouted after the runner who was clearly too full of his own importance to worry about her "you ignorant bastard!"

Angry, she lit a cigarette and carried on in the rain. It wasn't particularly cold, just horrible drizzly rain that coated her face having the only advantage of waking her up slightly and making her at least feel like she'd had a wash this morning. Carrying on past the Auditorium and the Leisure Centre Kerry, for some reason, reminisced about the ice skating discos she used to go to as a kid and wondered what some of the people she met there was up to nowadays. Then she thought she really should have done better at keeping in touch with people. A bang on her shoulder as a runner hit her, it was the same guy who nearly sent her flying outside her house.

"Fucking twat."

He turned around, breathless from running he looked at the floor.

"Err.....err....."
"The word you're looking for is sorry."
"Yeah.....err....erm.....sorry."
"There we go wasn't too fucking difficult was it?"
"Err.....no."

He ran away quickly taking a right up the loop of Cromwell Road while Kerry was going straight on. She recognised him but couldn't quite place where from. He looked a lot older than her so it wouldn't be from school and she surely would have remembered someone with a stammer as bad as that. He'd gone bright red too speaking to her, but he was kinda cute in that bad boy way Kerry had always been attracted to.

The Willows estate looked exceptionally grey in the dawn drizzle as Kerry continued her walk towards the cut through onto Great Coates before getting to the factory on the Pyewipe industrial estate. It filled Kerry with a sense of impending doom as a mixture of the gloominess of the estate, the dreariness of the weather, the sheer fact of having to work for peanuts in a fish factory for the rest of her life and her own tiredness drained any happy thoughts. She could almost feel her serotonin depleting - being shipped away to uncharted waters that she may never find. The runner had completed his lap of Cromwell Road and was coming past in the opposite direction. Seeing Kerry he looked down at the floor but Kerry gave him her friendliest and flirtiest smile which caused him to go an even brighter shade of red than before and Kerry chuckled to herself that if she could do that to him dressed like a minger with no makeup on and greasy plastered back hair then imagine what he'd be like when she was dolled up for a night out. Bless him she thought.

Eventually getting to the cut through Kerry gave her usual check over the shoulder that she did every morning, paranoid of being followed down the passageway ever since she was jumped and beaten up on the "black path" on the Wybers when she was at school. Satisfied that nobody was there she continued down the alley, upping her step rhythm just so that it was over with quicker. Halfway down she felt a sudden pain in the back of her head as she fell to the floor, looking up to see a man in a balaclava kicking her unconscious with one swift boot to the face.

Δ Δ Δ

Morris and Hughes pulled into the entrance of Diana, Princess of Wales Hospital and got out of the car. Coughing and spluttering Morris lit a cigarette, inhaling the smoke shallowly until the cough subsided.

"You really should think about giving those up Sir," said Hughes tentatively

"Who the fuck asked you?" Morris snapped his retort as Hughes stood in silence for the rest of the cigarette, pacing up and down much to Morris' annoyance.

Entering the hospital they were greeted by a uniformed officer who briefed them on the events and they were ushered into a side room where a doctor came to speak to them.

"We've had to give her seventeen stitches in her vagina, she's got internal injuries and will need an operation to realign her rectum and anus. She's still a little confused and concussed so please gentleman have a little decorum."

"Did you retrieve any semen?" asked Hughes

"No sorry, no signs of ejaculate."

"Fuck it!" exclaimed Morris.

Kerry was lying on the bed, aching all over and still confused. Struggling to breathe through her broken nose and a severe pain in her backside and her pussy. Two men, clearly police, walked in.

"I'm Detective Chief Inspector Morris, this is Inspector Hughes of Humberside police, can you tell us what you know."

"I know I'm in a lot of fucking pain, they tell me I've been raped but to be honest with you I was unconscious so I don't remember nothing, I was walking to work through the cut through, I got hit then he kicked me in the face."

"Did you see your attacker?"

"Only quickly and he had a balaclava on."

"Anything unusual or suspicious about your walk to work this morning?"

"Not really, oh a guy running."

"And could you identify this man?"

"Yes probably but I'm pretty sure, well I don't think it was him, no, erm....I don't know."

"Well what do you know?"

Kerry broke down in tears, she was confused enough without these policemen interrogating her. She felt like they had her under suspicion and they were going to arrest her for being unconscious while she was being raped. She felt like it was her fault he'd done that to her and that she was stupid for not remembering what he was wearing other than the balaclava, but she was sure he had different clothes on to the cute runner, or was she sure? The confusion made her break down in tears.

"Look I just don't fucking know alright?" She managed through the tears

"Come on now that's enough," the red headed nurse ushered the two detectives out of the room "she's clearly upset and you're just distressing her more."

Outside the room Hughes turned to Morris

"Reckon it's the beast?"
"Same hallmarks except not a park."
"Been a while though."

“Six years, but he’s been quiet that long before, just wish I knew why.”

“You know who got released yesterday don’t you?”

“Yeah, and she saw a runner, surely not though, not even he’s that fucking stupid.”

“You’ve always said he’d fuck up eventually.”

“You’re right, lets go nab the fucker.”

∆ ∆ ∆

“Morning Mrs. MacKenzie.”

“What the fuck you doing here? He was only released yesterday can’t you fucking leave him alone one fucking day to try and live his life?”

“Pleased to see you too Mrs. MacKenzie, is Steven in?” Morris took glee in seeing her squirm

“Come in you nasty pieces of work, Steven!”

Macca came down the stairs

“For fucks sake, what now?”

“Morning Steven, enjoy your holiday?”

“Is that all, you’ve come to gloat?”

"No Steven, let me cut to the chase. The cut through Cromwell Road to Station Road, a bit close to home for you isn't it?"

"I haven't got a fucking clue what you're on about."

"I think you do Steven, not even out a day and having to satisfy your filthy desires."

"What the fuck, I've told you it's not me a thousand fucking times."

"Steven MacKenzie I'm arresting you on suspicion of rape....."

∆ ∆ ∆

"Number 4 is definitely the guy I saw running" Kerry said from behind the one-way mirror, identifying Macca from the line up of similar sized men stood the other side "but I'm not sure he's the guy who attacked me"

"What makes you not sure?" An irate Morris asked in a tone of a man desperate for a conviction and unbefitting of a police officer.

“I just.....err.....I’m just.....err.....the more I think about it the more I’m sure.....err.....I think....that he wasn’t wearing the same clothes.”

“But you can’t be sure?”

“No as I’ve already told you it was a split second, I’m sorry I can’t help more I really am” the tears that had been almost constant in the weeks since the attack flooded back into Kerry’s eyes.

“Fine” Morris stormed out of the room certain that once again lack of evidence was going to hamper any chance he’d have of getting this bastard in front of a jury. The familiar sound of Morris taking out his frustration on the wall echoed down the corridor as he repeatedly punched the plaster. An equally as frustrated Hughes trying to calm him down.

# Chapter 28

Lucas noticed the change in Morris almost at once as he arrived into work this morning. The downtrodden demeanour of recent weeks seemed to have lifted and, at a push, it would be possible to say he almost seemed upbeat.

"Morning Sir."
"Morning Hughes, can I have a quiet word?"

This was usually a bad sign as it meant he was in for a bollocking of some shape or description but Morris' mood told him otherwise. Walking down the corridor they found a vacant interview room and went in.

"Look can I start by saying I'm sorry for my behaviour recently."
"Is it the be.....the MacKenzie thing Sir?"

Lucas caught himself just before breaking one of the new golden rules. Absolutely nobody was to name the case by the beast moniker and Lucas was sailing pretty close to the wind by daring to even mention Macca's name. They'd pretty much resigned themselves to the fact that with no solid DNA evidence that they were stuck in a rut as far as this case went, even though deep down they were both certain that they had the right man. When Lucas had suggested that maybe somebody might pull off the balaclava Morris had confused him by saying there was more chance of a wrestler breaking kayfabe and unmasking Kendo Nagasaki to a Memorial Hall full of pensioners.

"I've been busy doing some secret work with the Lincolnshire constabulary, we reckon we might be close to something big, really fucking big and very close."

"And why has it been in secret Sir?"

"I didn't know who I could trust in Humberside over this and I'm sorry I've excluded you."

"It's fine Sir, can I ask what it's all about?"

"A big drugs bust. We reckon we might have the region's biggest supplier."

"Ok and you think he might have friends on the force?"

"Not think, I know."

"And can I ask who it is?"

"Not yet Hughes, but you'll find out soon, we're hoping to do the raid today."

∆ ∆ ∆

There was an atmosphere of excitement buzzing around the station when news broke that something big was happening today. The shroud of mystery and secrecy of it all further stirred the enthusiasm of the officers chosen to take part.

"Under no circumstances must anybody not involved in this operation be told anything regarding this operation, is that understood? Absolutely nobody."

The room murmured in concordance with the instructions yet nobody dare speak up and ask what was actually going on. There was an acceptance that it was on a need to know basis and they were just there for numbers should anything tasty arise.

Pulling up in convoy Morris instructed officers to tape off an area as the lock up was crowbarred open. Inside was a rusty old Mini Cooper and not much else apart from a few shelves of power tools that looked like they'd been lifted from a shipment at the docks.

"Fuck it!" Cried Morris giving the tyre of the Mini a tremendous kick. The kick was so hard that rust dispersed from every panel of the car and caused the boot to fall open.

"Fuck me! There's thousands of them" said a detective from Lincolnshire "much, much more than we thought"

Morris' eyes widened like the proverbial child in a sweet shop as he stepped round the back to see thousands of individual paper wraps, a set of weighing scales and a holdall full of money sitting in the boot.

"Must be well over a kilogramme of smack there."
"And some."
"Six figures street value at least there."

Back at the police cordon two uniformed officers watched the detectives from Lincolnshire load the boxes of evidence into a car and lifted the tape to let them through while watching a coughing Morris light yet another cigarette using the tab end of the last one he'd just finished.

"Fuck me he's chaining them today," one said to the other.

"Probably the most excitement the old bastard's had in years."

"Yeah miserable old cunt needs to get his hole."

"I'm sure Hughesy would oblige."

"I know, little bender."

Within minutes a familiar face came into sight.

"Dave! You're meant to have fucking retired, miss us that much did you?"

"Yeah something like that, what you doing here?"

"Some dozy cunt has got a kilo of junk hidden in his lock up, I expect he'll be getting a knock on the door soon."

Dave turned and ran.

"Fucking stop him!" Morris screamed throwing his cigarette on the floor and setting off.

Lucas sprinted up the hill and hurdled the tape, leaving the uniformed officers still rooted to the spot wondering what the hell was going on. Running across the busy main street Davies got an edge on Lucas, who had to avoid traffic, but soon the younger man's fitness, stamina, gym sessions and cigarette free lungs paid dividends as he leapt on Davies back causing them both to go tumbling with Davies ending up on top.

"You cock sucking little queer," Dave sneered then spat in his face as he brought his right fist to Lucas' temple followed in quick succession by another to the cheek. He raised his hand to follow up with a third when he was rugby tackled away by Morris. Pulling him to his feet Morris put the cuff on Davies' right wrist as he read him his rights. Davies flung his head backwards catching an out of breath and unusually unsuspecting Morris on the nose, causing him to see stars and temporarily disable him long enough that Davies escaped his grasp. Running down the street with one hand in a handcuff Davies pushed past a young mother with a pushchair and ran for all his worth. He was spun around by a push on his shoulder, he saw Lucas stood in front of him. Davies grabbed Lucas by the back of the head and pulled him forward lifting a knee into his face, expecting him to fall to the ground Davies let his grip loosen. Lucas stood up and swung a punch connecting with Davies' jaw fracturing it and causing him to take a step back. Davies then doubled up as the wind was knocked out of him by a testicle rupturing knee to the groin.

"How you like that Dave? Beaten up by a fucking cocksucker?" Lucas angrily shouted over the prostrate Davies who was writhing in pain on the floor. Lucas was held back from putting the boot in by the uniformed officers who had eventually arrived on the scene as a recovered Morris finished his arrest and called for an ambulance.

# Chapter 29

Marc had had enough. He knew it was usual for mates to take the piss out of each other but this time they'd gone too far. He could take the jokes about his weight and his glasses but to make such vile remarks about his Aunt Val was bang out of order. Just because she didn't have any arms or legs because Nanna had taken thalidomide in pregnancy didn't make her any less of a human being and to joke about picking her up and using her as a "cum dump" had crossed the line. Even more so when Mike had spoken about fucking her in her ileostomy hole. Marc slammed down his pint so heavily that the glass had smashed all over the table. He didn't hang around in the Smugglers to see what the subsequent fall out was. Now, ten minutes later, he stood at the top of Ross Castle, tears in his eyes and still angry with those bunch of cunts, wishing he'd slammed the glass into Mike's fat fucking face. He'd ignored the texts and calls and had turned his phone onto silent and hid behind the wall as he watched them walk past, still laughing and joking with each other. "Fuck them," he thought as he binned the night in Meggies with them off for a session in Grimsby with his mates from college instead.

Scrolling through the missed calls and deleting the unread texts he dialled the taxi to take him into town.

"You go watch Town?" The taxi driver said to him

"Not very often mate, heard they won today though. 4-1 wannit?"

"Yeah, beat Barnet."

"You go?"

"No mate just listened to it on the radio, reckon Buckley's lost the plot to be honest, I ain't been since last time Buckley got the sack and we got all them foreigners under Lawrence. Too many scrobs and don't get me started on that Chinky."

Pulling round into Victoria Street, Marc, fed up of the right-wing views of the taxi driver (which typified the town) decided to walk the rest of the short journey to meet his friends in The Barge. The drink was in full flow by the time he got there, and Gilly decided Marc had to play catch up - loading him up with three shots of neat vodka and a bottle of strong Belgian lager. Feeling much better about the company Marc relaxed and was soon in the swing of the evening. He's already decided that nights out in future should centre on this group of friends rather than the piss-takers he'd left in Meggies. Besides, he preferred the rockier music in these venues. He looked at his phone to check the time, just gone 10, and deleted some more missed calls and texts of that other group of bastards. He had plenty of drinking time left and would not have his night completely ruined so he turned his phone off.

With his vision blurred from the drink and California Strut in his ears, the bright lights and an empty stomach signalled to Marc it was time to get a kebab. Devoid of any other thought he stumbled towards Victoria Kebab House feeling much drunker than he had for a good few months. Ordering his large donner he handed over what was left in his wallet deciding against a can of pop as funds were insufficient. Hiccuping as the fiery chilli sauce hit his alcohol sodden stomach Marc sat down on the pavement opposite the kebab shop and invented his own story lines of the passers by's lives and nights out. Chuckling to himself about the girl in the queue whom he had decided was definitely having an affair with her married boss, he shovelled handfuls of greasy chilli covered meat into his mouth, spilling sauce all down his front. Leaving half a kebab on the pavement, Marc stood up and staggered the 50 yards to the taxi rank trying to either cop off or push in front of the two girls in front of him. His drunken demeanour and chili covered top meant he was exceptionally unsuccessful at either.

The taxi smelt of stale diabetic sweat which made Marc heave, remembering he had no money, Marc made the alcohol fuelled decision to take the taxi to the other side of the park then do a runner. He'd done it before plenty of times in the past so why would tonight be any different, plus he fancied himself against the overweight blob driving.

"Taylors Ave please mate, near Trinity Road."

"Ok mate, Weelsby Road way best for you?"

"Either mate, whichever you think is quickest."

Adrenaline pumping as the cut through to Haverstoe Park drew closer, Marc sobered up just about enough.

"Just here will do mate."

The taxi stopped, Marc opened the door and sprinted down the road and into the cut through between the houses. Approaching the denser trees at the end Marc turned his head over his shoulder and noticed the fat taxi driver must have given up on running. Facing back the right way and still running at full pace Marc was knocked to the ground by a clothesline to the throat from a swinging arm by a man in a balaclava. Feeling a kick hit the side of his head, then another, then a painful boot to the kidney as he rolled into a ball to protect himself. Another kick in the back was swiftly followed to one to the head which made him briefly lose consciousness. The eerie silence should have been broken by his screams but nothing came out, his voice box apparently rendered unusable by the fear and the earlier punch to the throat. He felt the gravel of the path grazing his back turn into soft wet mud as the man dragged him by his legs. He tried to kick out, but the guy had hold of him too well and he opened Marc's legs and stamped down on his nether regions then his stomach. The pain intensifying with each kick as the numbing effect of the night's alcohol left his system. Being forcefully turned onto his stomach Marc tried to kick out again which was this time nullified by a stamp to the hamstring which broke his femur. All the heat in his body congregated on the broken bone and his leg went limp as he felt his face being forced into the ground by one hand and his jeans being ripped down by the other. A punch from behind into his balls caused him to be violently sick from the pain, which disappeared almost instantly being replaced by a searing pain like a red hot poker as his anus was fissured by the forceful entry of the man's cock. The violent strokes of his hips accompanied by blows to the back of the head as Marc's now limp body accepted its fate. Balls and cock being painfully and heavily manhandled by gloved hands.

The ordeal was over in minutes, yet to Marc it felt like a lifetime, prone and lifeless he lay on his front crying as he felt the blood from his ring piece dribbling down his testicles. Seeing his phone on the other side of the path Marc dragged his body towards it. The pains in his leg and arsehole were excruciating and getting worse with each and every movement. Eventually he reached his phone, crying while turning it back on and dialling 999.

ΔΔΔ

Morris and Lucas arrived at Haverstoe Park as Marc was being loaded into the back of the ambulance by the paramedics. Loaded up on Entinox he was only semi-coherent but the words "bloke", "rape", "arse" and "balaclava" were audible enough to send shivers down Morris' spine.

"He's never attacked a male before has he Sir?" Lucas asked with trepidation.

"No he's not and I'm not sure I like this one bit."

Following the ambulance to the hospital the talk soon turned to Macca.

"I'm not so sure he's gay though Sir."

"What would you know Hughes? A guy like that isn't going to announce it to us is he?"

Struggling with his words so to use to his homophobic superior Lucas tried to explain "gaydar" in his most straight friendly manner.

"You're telling me puffs can tell other puffs are queer?"

"Kind of Sir."

"Pull the other one it's got bells on it!"

"I'm being serious."

"And I suppose once you've sucked a cock you get this magic power do you? Haha I've never fucked a queer but my boyfriend has?"

Lucas decided that maybe keeping quiet was the best course of action. He'd come out to Morris kind of by mistake and he'd taken it a lot better than he thought he was but at the end of the day, Morris would never be a modern man and the jokes would probably never stop. The car was silent for about 3 minutes until Morris broke the silence.

"Maybe, just maybe."

"Maybe what Sir?"

"Now I'm not saying this is the case, but MacKenzie."

"Yes Sir?"

"What if he got turned on the inside?"

"What do you mean Sir? Turned gay?"

"Yes Hughes, what if?"

"What if what?"

"Ok so MacKenzie, used to being a big fish in a small pond, we send him to jail and he's no longer the biggest fish. But he wants to be the big fish."

"Erm ok."

"He upsets the wrong person and ends up being their prison bitch. It happens, a lot of lifers are prison gay."

"Ok but that's the other way round isn't it Sir?"

"Well yes, but maybe he got with a girl gay who wanted to be the taker and MacKenzie got the taste for being the boy, the giver, I don't know what terms your lot use. Is it possible?"

"I suppose Sir but it's a bit far-fetched isn't it?"

"It's all we've got. We'll interview the poor bastard in the ambulance once they've stitched his arsehole back together then we should go pay our Mr. MacKenzie a visit. I can't wait to see his face when a puffter like you accuses him of being a queer."

∆ ∆ ∆

"So Mr MacKenzie would you like to tell me where you were last night?"

"What's this? He can't get me to confess so you're having a go? He's the bad cop, you're the good cop? This should be a laugh."

"Answer the question please Steven, where were you at approximately 3 o'clock this morning?"

"Tucked up in bed with my teddy, I need my beauty sleep."

"Well we've got someone who has described somebody your height and body size in Haverstoe Park last night."

"Can't have been me, didn't even go for a run last night. Why has another girl been raped?"

"No."

"Why the hell you questioning me then?"

"It was a man who was raped, same way as all the girls, person fitting your description at the scene."

"Well it can't have been me I'm not a puffter, no offence."

"Nobody is saying you are Steven."

"Good, so why am I here?"

"Well you've just been in prison."

"Yeah I know that, what's that got to do with the price of fish?"

"Well you wouldn't be the first inmate to engage in sexual activities with another male because of lack of women."

"I'm not a fucking puffter."

"What I'm saying Steven is that maybe you got a taste of it inside and there wasn't any girls walking through the park last night."

"I'M NOT A FUCKING ARSE BANDIT ALRIGHT?" Macca slammed the table hard causing his lawyer to jump.

"We'll leave it here for the time being I think," Morris interjected.

∆ ∆ ∆

Morris and Lucas stood next to a timid Marc on the other side of the glass as the identification parade was escorted out of the room. Bound to a wheelchair for the foreseeable future due to the nature of the broken leg, Marc had identified two different people with and without the balaclava, neither of which were Macca. An irate Morris had tried to push him but Lucas had intervened as it was clearly causing too much upset to Marc. The lack of any clear evidence was once again hampering their investigations and neither of them liked it. Both certain it was Macca they escorted Marc away for debriefing with an air of dejection as they conjured a plan in their minds to catch the bastard once and for all.

# Chapter 30

A dangerous combination of tiredness, opiate withdrawal and trepidation made Ben's hands shake as he handed over the fake £10 notes to buy his train ticket. No longer being on supervised methadone had made it a lot easier to sell, not to mention more lucrative. He'd only been taking 40 of his prescribed sixty millilitres for a few weeks and not taken any for a few days, so much so that he had over 500ml to sell to French last night. That, along with a serendipitous dispensing error where the pharmacy had given him 4 weeks of diazepam instead of one and a much reduced heroin use (to almost none) meant that Ben was debt-free to French, and so much so that French was willing to pay him enough to cover the rest he required for the train fare. It was just Ben's luck though that French had insisted on paying it from the stash acquired through his latest venture of money counterfeiting. Trembling as the cashier handed him his orange and yellow ticket, a layer of sweat iced over Ben's back giving him goosebumps. Looking at the train station clock it was 7:03, about half an hour before his train left to take him back to Grimsby. He'd not seen this early in the morning for a long time and the lack of sleep through excitement was catching up with him - he needed some caffeine and he needed some form of opioid to take the edge off.

Handing the last of his fake notes to the lady in Boots, Ben collected his 32 Nurofen Plus and Red Bull and headed towards his platform. As the sugary liquid fizzed around his mouth, Ben swallowed, feeling it and the twelve Nurofen hit his stomach. This caused a borborygmus gurgle and a painful cramp as he sat on the carriage chair waiting for the codeine to relieve some of this current hell. Closing his eyes Ben thought quickly of giving this train journey a miss and heading over to see if French, or one of his associates, could fix him up but then the longing desire to return home, which had been eating at him more than the need for heroin, replaced those thoughts as his stomach cramped again and his sweat covered body spasmed.

"Are you ok love?"

Ben opened his eyes to a friendly looking woman.

"Errr yeah, where are we?"

"Just pulling out of Newark, you were having a nightmare I think, you were kicking and punching and screaming."

"God was I?"

"And look at you love, you're wringing wet with sweat. Are you sure you're ok?"

"Just a bit of the flu love, don't suppose you've got a drink have you?"

The woman passed Ben half a bottle of water saying he could finish it and sat down on the seat across the aisle from him. Surreptitiously, Ben popped out eight Nurofen and swallowed them down with the water. His stomach grumbled and gurgled again, almost in protestation to the onslaught of liquid and tablets. Ben's body cramping once more as he longed for a hit or even some methadone to see him right. The minuscule amount of codeine in the Nurofen just not quite satisfactory enough for his junk hardened opioid receptors as he pined for more and hoped the woman would now leave him in peace to continue this horrible withdrawal that he had bestowed upon himself.

∆ ∆ ∆

The pains in Ben's stomach were getting worse and he could barely move his legs from the cramp as he boarded the train to Grimsby at Doncaster station. "Just my luck," he thought to himself as he sat down on a carriage full of blokes who were clearly football hooligans. Trying to avert his gaze anywhere but at the group and keep his mind from the nauseating cramps in his stomach Ben's mind wandered off to what his motives were for returning to Grimsby. He had nowhere to live, no money, no idea who he knew there and most importantly no way of getting his precious drugs that would stop him feeling like this. Closing his eyes and trying to find the answers the griping pain getting worse Ben felt a heavy push on his shoulder.

“I’m fucking talking to you,” Ben opened his eyes to be confronted by a snarling boy of no more than 15 in a blue and white hooped Paul and Shark jacket and black cap. “I said I’m fucking talking to you!”

“Wh.....what mate?”

“Who do you support?”

Ben thought quickly as to why this would be a question to ask a stranger on a train and reasoned that any answer would probably be met with a fist to the face, especially as they were obviously going to Grimsby for the football.

“No one mate.”

“You don’t like footy, you a fucking queer or something.”

Ben kept silent.

“You scruffy bastard, I said you a fucking queer.”

The thought of getting beaten up made Ben’s adrenaline surge causing his already nauseous stomach to gurgle more. The youth was just about to unleash an attack when an elder guy in a very smart Aquascutum jacket pushed him away.

"Fucking leave it."

"But he's a rate scruffy twat Des."

"I said leave it, you draw attention to us here we'll get nicked or a reception from the plod when we get there, now leave him alone and calm down."

The elder gentleman, just identified as Des, beckoned for Ben to move over and sat next to him.

"Sorry bout that mate, one little sniff of ale and these young uns think they're Danny Dyer."

"Who?"

"Fuck me mate you are out the loop, heyar it looks like you could do with one of these."

Des magicked a can of lager from about his person, opened it and passed it to Ben. The last thing he needed right now was a beer but Ben took a grateful swig. The cold foam hitting his stomach caused yet another terrible gripe as the unbearable pain descended from his stomach through his intestines and to his rectum.

“You’re not really not into footy are ye mate?”

“No love the game just didn’t know what to say!”

“You’re Grimsby aren’t ye?”

“Yeah, long time ago though, a different time, a different place.”

“Always had respect for Grimsby, game bunch of fuckers, keep tryna tell these young uns they’re in for a busy day today but they ain’t for having it, think they’re invincible nowadays.”

“Didn’t we all?”

“Yeah, nothing a good kicking didn’t sort out though eh?”

“Haha you’re right there, who are you lot anyway?”

“Rotherham mate, you no idea of the fixtures anymore.”

“Been out of it too long.”

“Fair play mate, anyway I’ll leave you to it, enjoy the can.”

“Cheers mate.”

Des went back to his friends as Ben washed the remainder of the Nurofen down with the fizzy lager in the vain hope that the codeine might somehow kick in soon. The pain in his stomach getting worse and worse as the cramps in his arms and legs intensified to a point where normal movements seemed impossible. His head pounded and his sweat became icier as the train pulled into Scunthorpe. Ben reassured himself this meant not far to go, but he knew that the pain from this withdrawal might not subside as he alighted the train at Grimsby Town station. The pain in his stomach and intestines and rectum exacerbated as the panic of not knowing his immediate future for this afternoon and this evening set in. He could feel the acid rising up his gullet as his mouth filled with saliva and a metallic taste followed by a volume of warm lager flavoured acid accompanied by three undissolved tablets. Not wanting to cause a scene and not wanting to waste any codeine from the Nurofen Plus he swallowed the liquified vomit back down causing more agony to his already screaming insides. His arsehole started to burn as the docks came into sight, more anguish and suffering to him as every muscle and sinew felt icy cold yet fiery hot at the same time. His t-shirt and jeans wringing with sweat clung to his wiry heroin riddled frame as his outside iced over once more.

The train began to slow into Grimsby Town station, the familiar sights of his home town soothing Ben gently, the warm bosom of the motherland. Jerking and staggering his cramped up legs to near the door, Ben smelt the beer and felt the eyes of the youth element of Rotherham's supporters staring at him as they waited for the doors to open. Alighting the train and walking out onto Station Approach Ben's arsehole once again felt on fire, his body became covered in an icy sweat which was quickly replaced by a warm sensation up the small of his back and in his buttocks.

"The dirty bastard's shit himself! You scruffy smack head cunt! Yeah you, you scruffy bastard."

Turning round in a moment of confused clarity from his clouded thoughts, Ben was once again a 16-year-old football hooligan, out with his mates, protecting his home turf.

"At least I'm not a dirty Yorkie cunt" he screamed whilst trying to make his cramped up legs run towards the baying crowd. His body not letting him do what he wanted and needed to do Ben threw a slow motion dream punch as a right hook from the 15-year-old in the hooped jacket sent him tumbling to the deck. His side on fire as the Stanley knife blade drew a foot long gash.

"Rotherham Section Five you cunt" was sneered at him as a laughing gang rained a three-striped monsoon of varying sizes and colours of Adidas trainers on his torso and head. Drifting in and out of consciousness Ben only picked up snippets of sounds.

"Yorkshire, Yorkshire, Yorkshire.....

.

.

.

.

.....ambulance.....

.

.

.

.

.....in a bad way.....

.

.

.

.

.....WOOOOOOOOOOOOOOH.....

.

.

.

.

.....hello.....

.

.

.

.

.....hello, can you hear me?....

.

.

.

.

.....non-responsive.....

.

.

.

.

.....WOOOOOOOOOOOOOH.....

.

.

.

.

.....slap.....

.

.

.

.

......can't find a vein.....

.

.

.

.

......extremely dehydrated.....

.

.

.

.

.....intravenous drug abuser.....

.

.

.

.

.....oh my god! Ben.....

.

.

.

.

∆ ∆ ∆

Vikki was exceptionally tired spending her off time from shifts still at the hospital keeping vigil at the bedside. She'd held his hand while snoozing in the chair but he hadn't woken up. It had been three days now and still no response although he had squeezed her hand yesterday and she was certain he smiled earlier when she'd spoken to him. Her work friend Jenny popped her head in and offered to take her to the canteen for a cuppa. Vikki reluctantly accepted and went down the stairs and down the long corridor to the canteen. As Jenny bemoaned her tempestuous on-off relationship, Vikki felt silly as the words came out of her mouth explaining why this addict who had deserted her all that time ago (and had now been beaten up at the train station) meant so much to her, especially to the raging man-hater that was Jenny. Jenny's answer to most of Vikki's problems were that she should just taste the forbidden fruit of lesbianism with her but a chaste Vikki had never succumbed to her advances, making it very clear they were friends and only friends. Vikki felt the tears welling up as she recalled just how much Ben meant to her and although it was only a few months that those few months were the happiest she'd ever been.

Returning to Intensive Care Vikki was equally shocked and pleased to see the one eye that wasn't still swollen from the kicking open and sparkling that ocean blue that she loved so much. Twisted from a broken jawbone and with much fewer teeth than she was used to a somehow still familiar smile spread across Ben's face.

"Of all the gin bars in all the world."

"That won't work this time," an angry Vikki responded "you've had me worried sick and you've got a lot of fucking explaining to do."

# Chapter 31

The investigation room was a hive of activity as people broke away in individual conversations about Morris' idea. Lucas and Morris began an in-depth discussion about section 78 of the Police and Criminal Evidence Act and deciding that even if this was entrapment, it was their only choice to actually get evidence and nail this bastard once and for all. Besides, it was bloody difficult for any lawyer to argue rape as entrapment.

The plan was relatively simple, Morris had used all the past attack information to work out a date and possible location of the next one. All they needed was a female officer who could wander around the parks hoping to prey victim to this evil sod. Morris had the ideal candidate and Lucas, while surprised at the suggestion, agreed that it was a fantastic choice. Caroline, a brunette with a gym toned body, was an incorrigible flirt with an apparent insatiable appetite for sex, but most importantly an eye for detail which was going to make her a very good detective one day. When she got there, there would no doubt be accusations that she had slept her way up the ladder, but this would be unfair as she had been pretty indiscriminate as to who she'd slept with, and whilst not shagging the whole of the station she'd had more than her fair share. Morris liked Caroline as a person and he certainly fancied her body, he also enjoyed her flirting with him but to date they'd stopped there and Morris had assured himself not to take it further.

Approaching Caroline next time he saw her Morris exchanged pleasantries before asking

"How do you fancy doing some under cover work?"

"I've always wanted to get under your covers Sir."

"Come on, you know what I meant."

"Will it involve being close to you and that dishy partner of yours?"

"For an evening yes."

"Oooh just using me for one night Sir? You are a naughty one."

Δ Δ Δ

The evening of the proposed sting came around much quicker than Morris had anticipated and he was extremely anxious that preparations had not been anywhere close to meticulous enough for things to run as smoothly as he'd have liked. Sat in the passenger seat of the car with Lucas driving and Caroline in the back, Morris was worried that Caroline was dressed more like a high end escort than a local girl walking home from a night out in Cleethorpes. He was also having severe doubts if she had enough acting ability to pretend to be drunk and seriously considered getting Lucas to drive to the off licence and ply her with vodka.

"I feel really slutty, do I look slutty?" Caroline said breaking the awkward silence in the car. "What do you think Luke? Do I look slutty? Would you fuck me?"

Morris' guffaws to Caroline being obliviously unaware of Lucas' sexuality were childlike and unbefitting of a man of his age, experience and seniority but she had certainly broken the ice and ignited conversations that took all three of their minds off their nervousness. The talk continued in a similar vein as Caroline's trepidation seemed to enhance her flirtatious nature and made her border on the obscene, sometimes seemingly forgetting Lucas was in the car as she teased and attempted to woo Morris.

"Hey Sir, what do you call a police woman with a shaven pussy?"

"That's older than Noah! - cunt stubble."

"No Sir, you call her Caroline."

"Oh you naughty bitch."

∆ ∆ ∆

The dejection within the room overarched the whole station as their plan hadn't come to fruition. They'd not even had a sniff of an arrest for someone smoking weed or taking a piss in any of the parks. The depressive atmosphere stuck in Morris' throat as he resigned himself back to the drawing board and the vain hope that one day, just maybe one day, he'd eventually get a result on this one. The plan was a good idea he thought to himself, maybe he'd just miscalculated the day. The worse thing about this guy, he thought, was that he was too unpredictable, especially with the long gaps; sometimes years; between the attacks. He thought hard and as he sat at his desk, sighed deeply into the hands that rested over his face, holding back the tears of frustration. He felt a delicate hand placed on his shoulder and turned round to see a sympathetic smile on Caroline's face.

"It's been a long time since I've felt this slutty and not had a cock, fancy taking me home?"

# Chapter 32

Stood outside the hospital doors, Vikki cursed herself for starting again as she lit up a cigarette. She was annoyed and reasoned that she had every right to smoke when she was feeling this way. Annoyed and feeling stupid. She wasn't sure who she was angrier at, herself for trusting Ben, or Ben for betraying that trust. He had had nowhere to stay after being discharged and, in her clouded judgement, had offered her spare room despite his obvious problems and his Houdini disappearing act in London. She'd made it very clear they weren't a couple but the rush of butterflies in her stomach whenever he smiled at her and the satisfaction she got from the one stolen kiss last week reaffirmed to her that she very much still loved him. Her heart had broken last night when she found the burnt foil in the bin and Ben had broken down in tears pleading with her not to throw him out and begging for her help. She knew she must look like a mug to the outside world but her love for Ben and her caring, almost motherly, nature had taken over and she assured him that she would look after him but he had to promise to do it her way.

She'd spent most the morning neglecting her paid duties making frustrating phone calls and researching fruitlessly on the internet. There was a four month waiting list at the local methadone support clinic and she just did not have the strength nor the patience to support Ben for that long and she knew Ben would have no time for the religious ideology of the twelve step programme. They had one thing right though; he was certainly powerless over heroin. She had to think of a different way that would sort him out quickly and hopefully forever, she knew tough love wasn't the way forward even though she had contemplated slapping and shaking the living hell out of him.

Walking back through A&E Vikki nearly tripped over a box that had just been dumped in the corridor knocking it over in the process. "Bollocks" thought Vikki as she bent over to pick up the contents which had spilt all over the floor, thinking of the ear bashing she would give the stupid porter who'd left the box in such a daft place to begin with. Picking up the bits of paper and shoving them back in the box Vikki noticed something that could be her answer, a blank prescription pad already stamped with the hospital details. Her mind in turmoil between potentially helping the love of her life and getting the Ben she adored back and risking her professional career for it all, she slipped the pad into her pocket and continued cleaning up the mess. The dilemma continued to eat at her throughout the rest of her shift and the pad weighed heavy in her pocket as she walked to her car, her heart pounding in her chest as the guilt and the anxiety of being caught and the subsequent fall out raced through her mind.

Pulling up on her driveway, the decision still not fully made, Vikki opened the front door to find an extremely large bunch of flowers on the table with a note saying sorry but no sign of Ben. Immediately turning round and getting back in her car the desire to find him and make him safe was overwhelming.

△ △ △

Vikki had driven round Grimsby and Cleethorpes aimlessly for hours devoid of any ideas of where to even start looking for Ben. She'd tried all the parks she could think of and all of the old haunts she'd heard Ben talk of in the past but to no avail. Resigned to the fact he'd probably gone out of her life for good this time and, in spite of her best recent efforts, she had failed to keep him safe Vikki headed back home, tears welling in her eyes making driving difficult. Pulling in to the side of the road Vikki broke down sobbing, floods of tears streaming down her face as she gasped for air, the sadness escaping her body to be replaced by a sudden anger as she pummelled the steering wheel with her fists. "Bastard bastard bastard fuck!" she said in a whispered scream before continuing to lament both herself and Ben in a tirade of expletives. Lost in her own thoughts she pulled away from her parked position suddenly awoken by the thud of a cyclist's fist on the side of the car.

"Stupid fucking bitch!" the man on the bike whom she had nearly pulled out on screamed at her closed window. Winding the window down to apologise Vikki noted his Grimsby Town tracksuit top before inexplicably thanking the bewildered man and setting off for Blundell Park.

A lone figure sat on the kerb in the darkened car park in the shadows of the imposing Findus stand. He felt arms wrapping around him from behind and instantly felt secure as he rested his head on one of the arms.

"I'm so fucking sorry" he said without turning around to confirm the hugger's identity, a solitary tear running down his left cheek.

"No baby, I am. I will make it all better though baby."

"How princess?"

"Just promise me we do it my way."

"Anything."

∆ ∆ ∆

Vikki thanked Ben as he placed the mug of coffee in front of her. She'd spent most of the night awake thinking of just how to help him and felt tired. She thought to herself she must look like shit then glanced at Ben who was in the first stages of yet another withdrawal that it was now her mission to help him avoid. In her head it seemed so simple use the recently liberated prescriptions to prescribe Ben a steadily reducing regimen of opioids alongside a soothing course, obviously also reducing, of benzodiazepines. The reality was much starker. Firstly had anyone noticed the pad had gone missing and alerted the local pharmacies to be on the look out? That would mean a one-way ticket to the police station and the NMC fitness to practice committee. The second problem which entered her head was slightly easier to overcome, everyone had commented on how similar hers and Jess the junior doctor's handwriting was and she'd seen her signature enough times, plus there was a collection of the doctor's signatures circulated throughout the hospital so she just needed to get a copy and practice. Her third dilemma was that she needed some patient stickers to place at the top of the fraudulent prescriptions to make them look genuine, the process of liberating one from each patient she saw in her next shift would not only be laborious but fraught with the danger of getting caught and trying to explain her actions. Vikki's final conundrum was certainly the most difficult, there was no chance on earth the local A&E would prescribe methadone so that was out of the question straight away, the only option was to find a suitable replacement but then there might be questions raised when the information was collated and there had been a spike in prescribing of one item and she'd couldn't do it all at one pharmacy, no she thought, she needed to do this cleverly. It would take some Oscar winning acting and a lot of foot work and mileage around the town but Ben needed her, and this was the least she could do for her man.

Seizing her opportunities during her next shift Vikki's pockets now contained several patient identification stickers, the list of sample doctor signatures and, thanks to some stomach curdling flirting she had had to do with the repugnant pharmacist from the information department, a comprehensive list of various prescribable opiates and there relevant potency to one another.

Ben watched mesmerised as Vikki sat at home that evening with a pen, paper pad, calculator and BNF converting all the drugs she considered safe enough to procure on prescription to their equipotent dose of his most recent 40mg of daily methadone and then meticulously worked out exactly how many tablets of each drug and each strength she would need for him to take over her 8 week plan and hopefully free himself. He felt the first cramps and icy sweat of withdrawal almost leave his body in relief that this girl, this woman, the woman that changed his perception of the female form, his first true love, was willing to risk it all to help him and her plan was going to be put into action beginning first thing tomorrow morning. He stood up and went over to her to give her a thank you hug which culminated in a passionate kiss and a retreat to the bedroom where he mustered enough stiffness to make love to her and bring her to a shuddering climax. Faking his own satisfaction Ben contently lay in Vikki's embrace as they drifted off to sleep ready to embark on a new period in their lives once Vikki had got his first prescription tomorrow.

Sat in her car in the car park adjacent to Ronnie Ramsden's Vikki tore a prescription from the pad, not wanting to push her luck at the first attempt she selected an elderly patient from her array of identities and wrote what she considered to be a fairly innocuous prescription.

Paracetamol tabs 500mg
1-2 qds prn
100

Codeine tabs 30mg
1-2 qds prn
56

Signing it with her practiced moniker Vikki held it up and admired her handy work. Even if she did say so herself it was mightily impressive, so much so that even she would have acted upon the instructions had they been written on a chart at work. With an air of slight arrogance at her splendid forgery skills but with an overwhelming sense of nervousness in case she was about to get caught she strolled into Ramsdens and round to the pharmacy unit where she handed over her "Nanna's" prescription from the hospital. Her heart nearly jumped out of her mouth when the assistant asked her to fill out the exemption declaration on the reverse and her ring-piece fluttered with over-wroughtness as the worry of the handwriting on the front and back of the prescription being compared to one another dawned on her. She made a mental note to be more aware of this, especially if she was going to act as though these prescriptions were for family members and that she must remember to use nom-de-plumes when signing the information on the back.

With a boot now full of opiates and superfluous pain killers, laxatives and anti-emetics prescribed so as to not draw attention, a cocky Vikki wrote her next prescription, remembering her training as best she could.

Pethidine tablets 50 (fifty) mg
1 (one) prn for obstetric pain
Please supply 10 (ten) tablets

Handing it over at the counter Vikki retired to the comfort of the seats in the waiting area. She had been to practically every chemist in Grimsby and Cleethorpes and was now hungry and thirsty and had a headache which she assumed was being induced by her own personal withdrawal from caffeine. The inexplicably long wait for this prescription to be finalised and given to her in her hand filled Vikki with dread, especially when she saw the pharmacist talking animatedly on the phone. She expected the door to be flung open by policemen increasingly with each passing minute. Eventually the pharmacist shouted out the name she had chosen for this prescription which she had almost forgotten in the 15 minutes since she had handed it over. Standing up to acknowledge the call she made her way to the counter.

"There's a slight problem I'm afraid"

Fuck thought Vikki, they're on to me, I'm sure I wrote the prescription properly.

"Ok it's for my sister, she's already in labour."

"Oh not good then, the ones we've got in stock are out of date you see."

"Oh right, can't you give me those anyway?"

"No sorry I'm not allowed. I've rung around some pharmacies for you and they've got them in at Ramsdens."

"Oh right, thank you."

Shit thought Vikki, there was no way that anyone could be naive enough to believe someone's Nanna and pregnant sister were seen by the same doctor at the hospital on the same day. She decided that she probably had enough drugs anyway so returned home to give a very ill looking and clammy Ben his daily dose from her plan.

"Thank you, love you," he said as he washed the tablets down "I promise I'll do this."

# 2017

# Chapter 33

It was brightening up on Laceby Manor golf course as the sound Fred's club head made as it connected perfectly with the ball on the 12th tee resonated in Morris' ears. He stood in awe and appreciation of Fred's drive. The ball had landed perfectly on the fairway and Morris checked the Whole in 1 app on his iPhone and estimated that the 66-year-old Fred had just driven well over 250 yards on the par 5.

"How the hell you manage to hit like that?" A deflated Morris already 6 holes down asked.

"Retirement my friend! Being able to come here whenever I want. You can't be long off now?"

"Four months, can't wait!"

Continuing the conversation right on to the 18th green the men agreed that Morris had had quite an impressive career and whilst Morris had expressed anguish at never catching the rapist Fred had reassured him that not even literary greats such as Poirot or Sherlock Holmes could have got their man with such little evidence, besides there hadn't been an attack for over nine years.

Fred had another round that afternoon and Morris needed to do his supermarket shop so they agreed they should limit themselves to just the two in the clubhouse. Halfway through the second Morris' phone rang with the caller ID identifying Lucas was ringing. Apologising to his friend before sliding the screen to answer Morris looked deep in thought as the conversation transpired. Fred watched on as Morris became more hushed and the colour drained from him, becoming ashen before returning to an angry red.

"And why the fuck have they waited so long to tell us?" Morris angrily asked into his phone. "Don't do anything else, I'm on my way in."

"Trouble at the mill?" asked an inquisitive Fred.

"You could say that!"

"Oh dear."

“Well you know how I said it had been over 9 years?”

“Yeah.”

“We’ll make it 9 hours, an attack last night but no bastard has decided to tell me until now.”

Seething as he arrived at the station it was clear to Morris that his anger was shared by Lucas as he walked in on him asserting his authority in the case to one of the other detectives.

“All the same M.O. and a balaclava,” he said to Morris without offering as much as a hello.

“Let me guess there’s no fucking evidence again?”

“Of course not. It’s the same bastard I can feel it.”

“MacKenzie?”

“MacKenzie.”

# Chapter 34

Thankfully catching herself before anyone else, Jenny averted her lustful gaze from Vikki's bum and carried on with her work. Vikki really did have a nice arse and the uniform, although designed for practicality over fashion, stressed its finer qualities to Jenny. She was sure this wasn't just rebound lust from her and Alice breaking up yet again and she bemoaned Alice internally for breaking her heart yet again. Jenny had made no secret of the fact she fancied Vikki but, other than that drunken finger in the toilets on the works Christmas night out, Vikki was definitely straighter than an arrow and had amicably deflected any of Jenny's advances.

"Break time while it's quiet" Vikki said to Jenny motioning an invisible cigarette to her lips "you coming?"

Jenny never needed to be asked twice to have a break so promptly left what she was doing and joined her friend on their march to the smoking area.

"You seem a bit quiet today Vik, you alright?"
"Yeah it's just Ben,"
"He gone walkabout again?"

Vikki and Ben's relationship was a strong one, and they were both very much in love but the demons of Ben's past often weighed heavy in his mind and guilt-ridden he'd sometimes leave their house for a few days to "get his shit together" and then return a refreshed guy. He'd not touched so much as a co-codamol since Vikki had weaned him off the heroin and was nine years clean. Vikki trusted him enough to know he was probably just sofa surfing at his old mates from school or college and having a drink or two and certainly not mixing in any circles where temptation of either his heroin or, god forbid, his other old addiction to sex would rear their ugly heads. He'd admitted to sleeping rough a few times just to appreciate what she had done for him and to remind himself to how things might have been without having her love. This time, but, he'd stayed put but his behaviour was deeply concerning. She was certain, although couldn't be one hundred percent sure, that he'd developed a gambling addiction. Well maybe not a full blown addiction, but it certainly wasn't natural to be able to tell you the average number of corners a team in the Slovenian under 21 league concedes.

Confiding all this to Jenny just seemed so silly that she felt the anguish building up inside when she heard the words coming out of her mouth. As always Jenny had a rational explanation for Ben's erratic behaviour as she explained her thoughts on Ben's mental well-being and borderline obsessive compulsion which was, in her eyes, clear with a lot of his actions. It was also definitely not the action of an addict to be so open about their behaviour and if there was a problem, then she would have noticed financially and Ben would, almost certainly, be hiding it from her. Telling her not to worry, Jenny gave Vikki a big hug and then said "come on let's get back to work, I know you two will be ok, you've been through worse and you're destined to be together forever."

# Chapter 35

For nearly the entire train journey Tim had sat there with his earphones in but no music actually playing. He played with his phone occupying his mind with anything other than the actual reason for his journey. He contemplated texting Gina, but she'd be asleep now she had moved to Australia with her new boyfriend. Instead he watched the rain run diagonally across the window as the combination of the train's speed and gravity fought against one another as to who was the strongest force acting on the rain drop. His inner child painting its own imagery - the sideways movement was Hulk Hogan and the downward movement The Earthquake battling the rain drops as though they were in the "squared circle" for tonight's main event. Tim's imagination running away with itself as he then tried to recall as many of the headline WrestleMania events from when he was a kid as he could. The image of the Mr T and "Rowdy" Roddy

Piper boxing match soon changing him to challenge his brain to put the Rocky films in order. He was soon hurtled back into reality as he pictured Ivan Drago saying "if he dies, he dies" and it took every ounce of his being to not publicly break down in tears on this packed train.

He'd never had the best father-son relationship with Bobby but the old wino was still his Dad at the end of the day and when a distraught Karl had rang yesterday evening his first reaction was to head back home and make whatever peace was needed to be made before the inevitable happened. Plus it was obvious Karl needed him to do his elder brother duties now more than ever.

Taking time away from his thoughts just long enough to flick the V's at the passing Glanford Park Tim text Karl to let him know he'd be home soon and could he get Ray to come and pick him up at the station. He then realised what a funny concept home was and that Marvin Gaye was talking bollocks and peddling a myth, substantiated in part by Paul Young.

He hadn't "laid his hat" in Grimsby for over 20 years but it was, and always would be, unmistakably home.

Getting off the train at Grimsby Town station a sense of relief washed over Tim as he saw Ray's friendly face and Tim gave Ray a warm embrace as he cried softly, building up to a crescendo of sobs. This took Ray by surprise as they'd had no physical contact in the past, not so much as a handshake, and although by rights he was the boys "step-Dad" he knew he was viewed as their Mam's fella in their eyes.

"Come on," Ray said, stopping short of saying son "let's get you home, your Mam and Karl can't wait to see you,"

In true fashion of any Northern mother on the return of her prodigal son the dinner table was stacked high even though it had barely touched 11 in the morning. Almost crushing him with a vice-like bear hug she kept repeating how good it was to have "her baby" home and how much he needed to look after our Karl. She was right, Karl looked like he hadn't slept for a decade when he came into the room, obviously shell shocked from the sights he had witnessed only yesterday. After a quick embrace Karl recollected the events, he'd gone into the Jube for a swift pint after work and Bobby wasn't there. Knowing straight away something was wrong he'd gone round to Dad's place and got even more worried when there was no answer. He'd let himself in with his key and found Bobby lying on the bathroom floor.

"I can't describe the colour, like really yellow but really grey at the same time, if he wasn't talking to me I'd swear he was dead,"

"Christ so you rang an ambulance?"

"Yeah, then he says to me 'Karl I'm not feeling too clever' and the next thing I know there's fucking blood spewing out of him like the fucking Exorcist, his bathroom looked like that scene from Carrie man, it was fucking horrible it made me boke everywhere,"

"Jesus Karl!"

"I know,"

"So what was it? Did they say?"

"Yeah, they used some big long words but basically he had a varicose vein at the top of his gullet from the drinking and it had burst open,"

"Fuck me!"

"I know right? And anyway because of the booze his liver's knackered and his blood's too thin they said if I hadn't called the ambulance before then he'd have probably bled to death,"

"Jesus Christ Karlos it's a bloody good job you went round,"

"Think I just delayed the inevitable, the docs said his liver is absolutely fucked and not to hold out much hope of him coming home" Karl began to cry, the first time he had done since finding his Dad in such a state, Tim put a brotherly arm around him then forced his face into his chest as the tears continued to flow.

Composing themselves they tucked into the veritable banquet of sandwiches and related picnic food Mum had prepared as Karl filled Tim in on all the real information about the local stories that reading the tellywag website would never get you before saying.

"Oh when I was at the hospital I got speaking to that ginger bird who used to be in your form at school,"

"Vikki Smith? Cracking arse,"

"Yeah that's the one, well she's a nurse at the hospital and you'll never guess who she's shacked up with"

"Go on"

"Only Ben fucking Evans,"

"God, I've not heard off that cunt since he disappeared in London. Don't suppose you got his number did you?"

"No mate sorry didn't think what with Dad and all"

∆ ∆ ∆

"Mr. White, your father is in a terrible way"

"Yeah, I understand that so what's the situation Doc?"

"Well not only has he got the oesophageal varices that caused the bleeding he scores over 40 on the 'MELD' test,"

"I haven't got a clue what that means pal,"

"Basically there's a 3 in 4 chance he won't see out three months unless he gets a transplant,"

"Fucking hell, sorry Doc,"

"Once, if, we get him stable we'll transfer him to the specialised liver unit in Leeds but to be quite honest

I've never seen liver failure like this and I'll be surprised if he sees out this week,"

"Thanks Doc, we tried and warn him about the drink."

Stood with Karl in the smoking shelter after seeing the bloated lifeless heavily sedated shell that contained his Dad, Tim saw Vikki and a quite manly looking colleague walking towards them. He exchanged pleasantries and got Ben's number of her as she said he'd definitely be pleased to hear from him. He unlocked his phone, opened WhatsApp and sent Ben a message. He then sent a message to Ian back in Manchester.

Gonna be here a while mate, do us a solid and feed the cat

# Chapter 36

The fact Grimsby town centre had changed, and not necessarily for the better, was the main topic of conversation as Ben and Tim chatted like friends who saw each other only yesterday, ignoring the 18 years it had actually been. They sat in the newly re-opened Gulliver's, which was as far removed from the old place as could be. The only thing that really remained was the name and location as all the character of the dark, mirrored room had been replaced by a brightly lit identikit cocktail bar. Gone too were most the people who'd made the place what it was, and to be quite honest, although finished to a high standard, you could have walked out and ended up in any high street in Britain. They thought of moving on but Karl had just returned from the bar with new drinks and Vikki's friend Jenny was coming to meet them after cutting short a disastrous date. A sex starved Tim's ears had pricked up at the thought of a potential liaison with

Vikki's friend but any thoughts of getting laid tonight quickly dissipated as the obviously gay, masculine figure of Jenny arrived on the scene.

All getting along well, the group continued their assault on the cocktail menu with some gusto, the conversation getting louder and coarser as the inhibitions were loosened and jaws lubricated by the alcohol. The talk descended to a silence as the attention of the three single parties; Tim, Karl and Jenny; focussed on the parade of arses that walked past from a group of heavily intoxicated girls.

"God, I could eat that one in the blue" Jenny commented as the rest of the table looked round, identifying the girl as "Gemma the slag" from school.

"Mmmm I like straight slags" said Jenny clearly inebriated from too much wine at her date.

"Pretty much everyone at school had her," added Vikki to the conversation.

Ben and Karl exchanged a knowing glance before Jenny interrupted. "Even you three?"

“Not me” answered Tim smugly, knowing the story and loving seeing the anguish grow on Ben’s face who clearly didn’t want to be having this conversation. “had a chance but turned it down”

Karl had picked up on Ben’s erratic behaviour and was laughing to himself, bordering on maniacally. “Err.... I had a threesome with her” he spluttered, enjoying watching Ben’s face turn redder almost as much as his brother.

“Two guys or two girls?” Asked Vikki and Jenny simultaneously.

“Two guys, I, errr we, errr me and Gemma were much younger and inexperienced compared to the other guy,”

“Dirty bitch”, again simultaneously but with much different tones in their voice. Vikki one of disdain while Jenny one of lust.

“Yeah but the other guy, it was like, errr it was like he, you know, errr, corrupted us,”

Tim burst into fits of laughter, the angry look on Ben’s face and the look of awe on the two girls taking in the story was too much to bare and he couldn’t take anymore. The laughter building inside of him was exacerbated when Jenny asked the most innocent of questions.

"What about you Ben?"

Tim spurted drink out of his mouth "Yeah Ben did you?"

Karl, not wishing to miss a trick, threw his tuppence worth in "Yeah Ben?"

"You're a pair of fucking bastards!" Laughed Ben as he was forced to corroborate Karl's story and name himself as the older corrupter in the threesome. Vikki aghast at her boyfriend's revelations whilst Jenny, seemingly becoming more turned on, probed to find out minute details of the sordid ten minutes of action before just saying "dirty bitch" while licking her teeth and looking lustfully over to where Gemma was drinking.

Gemma eventually came over and said "hi" to everyone, giving Tim a frosty reception after he'd knocked her back a few years ago, flirting with Karl as an unsuccessful way of trying to make Tim jealous, she was, however, succeeding in getting Jenny going even more than she already was.

"That little slag is getting it tonight" Jenny thought to herself as she masterminded how to get some time alone with her. The opportunity didn't take long to arise as Gemma got up to go to the toilet, following her Jenny's eyes were transfixed on her arse as she thought what she could say. She didn't need to think hard as Gemma opened the conversation.

"Sorry we weren't properly introduced, I'm Gemma,"

"Oh I know, I'm Jenny, I work with Vikki,"

"Well hi..... so can I ask you something?"

"Of course."

"It's a bit personal,"

"I don't mind,"

"Are you gay?"

"Isn't it obvious?!"

"Well yeah,"

"Why you ask?"

"Well I've always been curious."

Jenny forced her tongue down Gemma's throat and pushed her into the cubicle as she reciprocated the kiss. Locking the door skilfully behind her without breaking contact. Her hands squeezing and caressing the arse that first drew her attention to Gemma before swiftly moving round to the front and sliding up Gemma's thighs, lifting her skirt with her wrists as her fingers stroked at a damp knicker gusset. An inexperienced Gemma tried to play with Jenny's A-cup boobs, pawing at them and trying to tweak her nipples. Jenny's hands working inside Gemma's panties to reveal a smooth pussy with slightly protruding labia and an exceptionally engorged clitoris, teasing the man in the boat out before expertly parting the labia to and sliding fingers inside, hitting her G-spot almost instantly. Using the heel of her hand to rub the clit as her fingers manipulated Gemma's zones inside it wasn't long before Gemma breathed deeply and heavily.

"Tell me you're a slag" Jenny whispered into Gemma's ear, nibbling on her lobe and kissing the nape of her neck.

"I'm..... a..... fuck.... ing..... dir.... ty.... SLAG!" panted Gemma as Jenny felt her explode on her palm.

"You're coming home with me tonight slag aren't you? There's plenty more where that came from" Jenny kissed Gemma's cheek then licked her hand clean seductively before egressing out of the cubicle and back to the table, winking at Vikki as she sat down.

Δ Δ Δ

Gemma was a bag of nerves in the taxi, she had always been curious and the toilet session was amazing, but she didn't know what was expected of her now and she didn't know whether she'd be any good. With boys she knew exactly what to do and had developed several skills but now a novice with an experienced dominant hand she felt uneasy but extremely excited especially when, with no shame in front of the taxi driver, Jenny declared she was going to treat her like the slag she was and give her a dam good fucking.

Taking Gemma upstairs Jenny allowed her a passionate kiss on the bed before removing her clothes with desire, lust and gusto. Bringing her to climax again with her fingers she then allowed Gemma to explore her body with her hands and play with her pussy. For a first timer she wasn't at all that bad and would have brought her to orgasm had she not kept changing position and rhythm at crucial moments. Needing more Jenny got off the bed and took her box of toys out from the divan. Choosing an 18 inch purple gel double ended dildo and a bottle of lube she took her place back on the bed and opened Gemma's legs. Her soaking wet pussy swallowed the dildo as Jenny eased it into her and made some liquid ooze out, it wasn't long before Gemma had taken it further than half way but could handle no more. Positioning herself at the other end Jenny caressed more lube onto the purple tube and slid her own pussy onto it, positioning her legs so that the girls vaginas were touching and each other's pelvic floor movements caused tremors down the dildo pleasuring the other girl. Jenny ground down hard, rubbing her clit against Gemma's groin. She wanted Gemma to tell her what a slag she was again but the words would not come out as she rode herself to an almighty orgasm.

"I wanna fuck you now slag" she said after composing herself. By now Gemma, weak from multiple orgasms was only too willing to comply as

Jenny returned to her box of tricks and pulled out a thick strap on with an internal vibrator. Adjusting the belts so both the vibrator and the phallus were secure and in the correct position she beckoned Gemma on to all fours. Slapping her arse hard she forced the fake penis hard into Gemma's pussy all the way to the hilt before rocking her hips hard and long so that Gemma felt each stroke hard. She slapped her arse hard once more and began to pull her curly brown hair.

"You're a proper fucking slag aren't you?" She sneered before slapping Gemma round the back of the head. "I fucking said aren't you?"

"Yes I'm a slag" replied a Gemma who wasn't sure if this pain was still pleasurable.

"You know what slags get don't you?"

"Punished?"

"Fucking yes they do, I'm going to rape your slutty arsehole you filthy slag" Jenny pulled out the dildo and rammed it into Gemma's arse. The force and depth of the gyration and the lack of additional lube caused searing pain for Gemma as her sphincter tore slightly.

"I'm fucking raping you now slag,"

"Please stop,"

"Mmmm Yes say that again slag,"

"Please stop" tears welled in Gemma's eyes.

"Call me the beast slag, fucking call me the fucking beast."

# Chapter 37

She'd been funny with him ever since the story came out about him, Karl and Gemma the other night. He'd tried to reason with her it was 20 years ago and it was before he'd fallen in love with her but she was seething after they'd got home and nearly a week later he still hadn't had so much as a peck on the cheek off her. In his old life he never would have had such hassle off a woman as one would never existed but now it just seemed lovely that she cared so much that this had upset her and in a perverse way he kind of liked it. He had thought about leaving her alone for a few days to calm down but had thought better, the last thing he needed was to alienate her even further so he decided against it. Although he was trying his best to thaw the frosty receptions and icy silences, he wasn't going to turn down the opportunity of a pint in the 'Sheaf on a Friday night with Tim while his oldest friend was still in Grimsby, and anyway he was only going to have a couple, Well maybe four or five, then get a taxi home.

Nine pints later and a good chinwag stood on Welholme Road he said his goodbyes to Tim reasoning it was going to be much cheaper in two separate taxis than one to Wybers via New Waltham or vice versa. Besides, he fancied a walk around People's Park to clear his head and sober up a little just in case she was still awake and argumentative. Walking down past his old flat he reminisced of older happy times spent there. Not necessarily happier times than when he and Vikki were good, but a different sort of happy and one definitely worth remembering.

Entering the park he smiled as he remembered girls from Gulliver's which he had taken there to fornicate with before he'd got the flat. He remembered a few faces and distinguishing features; such as the girl with three moles like Mickey Mouse on her bum; but struggled with names. Lying on the floor of the bandstand smoking his last cigarette, he closed his eyes, inhaling and exhaling deeply, enjoying the nicotine entering his system, and for the first time since trading his guitar to French for a hit he began writing song lyrics in his head. His mission first thing tomorrow, he thought, would be to buy a cheap second hand guitar and place the chords and melody to his new poem. He was startled and rudely interrupted by an amorous couple of late teenage appearance who obviously wanted to use the bandstand to further their carnal knowledge of each other. The boy was visibly shocked and shaken by his maniacal cackle as he remembered bribing a tramp with cigarettes to leave the exact same bandstand for the exact same reason all those years ago, only to be caught by the barman from the Wheatsheaf on his way home from work. As he left, he wished the couple good luck before asking to bum a fag, thus completing the revolution of this ironic circle of life. He hoped that one day this young apprentice would repeat such a venture to support balance and equilibrium in the universe.

Walking past the lake he paused briefly to take the lighter out of his pocket, sparking up the cigarette, a much cheaper and stronger brand than his own, he closed his eyes to savour the first inhale. A sharp pain hit the back of his head as he was knocked to the floor and dragged to the bushes by the gloved hands of a balaclaved man.

# Chapter 38

"He's either getting more brave or more stupid" Morris said to Lucas in the car driving to the hospital. There hadn't been two attacks in the same month before let alone on consecutive nights "maybe he wants to get caught".

The attacker had violently assaulted a young lady who had been out in Cleethorpes celebrating a friend's birthday. The lack of available taxis had meant the friends had walked home together, and the attack had happened within minutes of them going their separate ways. Details so far had been sketchy, but the girl had tugged on the balaclava briefly enough to see her attackers nose which was a lot more than they'd had previously.

Arriving at the hospital, Morris lit his cigarette. It suddenly struck Lucas that he hadn't seen Morris smoking for nearly three years, yet here he was outside the hospital doors doing so in his trademark fashion before going to interview a rape victim. The police doctor ushered them into the side room, as was the protocol, to brief them.

"We recovered a condom out of her severely lacerated vagina,"

Morris' eyes widened like saucers as the letters D, N and A circled round his brain.

"So no condom means that we've got a semen sample yes? Please tell me you followed procedures for maintaining the integrity of the sample."

"That's the thing; there was no semen, not even a trace of it. We've given the condom to the lab already"

"Fuck it!"

Δ Δ Δ

"We'd normally expect to find some Cowper's fluid inside the condom even if there wasn't an ejaculation but nothing" said the voice from the lab at the other end of the phone "not even a pubic hair to try and extract something from. All we can tell you is that, from the fibre sample we took from her nails, the balaclava was made of an acrylic wool blend,"

The iPhone's screen shattered as it hit the wall moments after being launched from Morris' hand.

"How the fuck can the fucking condom come off and there still not fucking be any fucking DNA?!" He screamed aggressively at Lucas before his hand disappeared through the wall sending dust and shards of plasterboard in all directions. If there was a section in the Guinness Book of Records for the amount of times fuck could be said whilst punching a wall in a minute, then Morris would have been meeting Norris McWhirter and Roy Castle pretty soon.

∆ ∆ ∆

Outside the interview room Morris and Lucas scoured the selection of pictures of eyes and noses that they were about to show the latest victim. They had both correctly identified Macca without a second glance, Morris reasoning it was because he had fantasised putting his head through it on too many occasions. They entered the room and talked to a timid and still petrified young lady.

"Take your time and if you recognise any, please let me know" said Morris sub-consciously tapping Macca's nose when saying the words.

The girl looked, and looked, and looked a third time and just shook her head and started to cry. Taking the pile of pictures back off her Morris selected Macca's and slid it back on the table.

"Are you absolutely sure?" He said in a voice far more threatening than the situation warranted. He wanted to pick up Macca's picture and shove it in her face and say "this one!"

"I'm sorry, none of them, this guy's was more, err less, err..... less..... broken,"

Morris' metacarpal fractured as his big fist made yet another dent in the corridor wall.

"Fuck,"

# Chapter 39

Robert "Bobby" White's body eventually gave up its fight, and he exhaled his last breath on the High Dependency Unit of Diana, Princess of Wales Hospital at 11:21. His sons, Tim and Karl, were at his bedside as his soul left the bloated yellow body and peacefully transcended to another plain. Nothing was said and no tears shed for fifteen minutes until the elder brother tapped the younger on the back and suggested a cup of tea, swearing by their mother's mantra that there was no problem in the world that couldn't be solved by a cuppa.

Walking down to the hospital cafe they passed a fraught looking Vikki who was having the shift from hell.

“He’s gone” Tim said to her through his own bizarre sympathetic smile, expecting tears to flow which weren’t forthcoming.

“Sorry to hear that”

“Can you let Ben know?”

“Course I can sweetheart” she said giving him a big hug.

They continued their walk down the long corridor to the busy cafe where they bought their tea and went to look for a seat. Macca’s Mum was sat alone at a table with 3 empty chairs so they went to join her.

“Hi Mrs. MacKenzie” said Tim turning on his well-practised charm which he reserved for parents back in the day.

“Hi Tim, Hi Karl, you here to visit your Dad? I’ve heard about him, sounds horrible, I’m here with our Hannah, but for me, I’m at the rat poison clinic for my blood clot,"

“Yeah” said Tim. Before he could start to tell Mrs. MacKenzie about his Dad she had interrupted him with her quick-fire incessant talking.

“Oh our Hannah will be pleased to see you, she’s outside having a fag, but she’ll be here soon, she’s always telling me how you’re both getting on and what you’ve posted on Facebook and stuff,"

“Fuck” thought Tim. Hannah’s friend request had been sat on his Facebook for five years, too cowardly to accept yet not having the heart to decline. As far as he knew, and the look on his face confirmed, Karl wasn’t friends with her on there either. He really must be more careful with his privacy settings he thought.

Hannah arrived. She was wearing her hair up and looked like she hadn’t slept for months. Dressed in a vest and trousers which (if one were to be unkind) were more akin to pyjama bottoms. She was wrapped in an oversized cardigan which did not flatter her shape but gave her the comfort she desired as she pulled the sleeves down further using a hole she’d cut in the cuff for her thumbs to slide through. Her face looked not as though she’d seen a ghost (well two ghosts) but more that those ghosts were defecating on her table.

"Hey Hannah" Karl, obviously the braver (or least informed) of the brothers, broke the silence.

"Karl" Hannah's voice was icy, numbed by a combination of shock from seeing these horrid men and high strength anti-psychotic injections.

"How you doing?"

"I was OK until I saw you two."

"Oh Hannah it is good to hear you joking with your friends," Mrs MacKenzie, unaware of the reality of the statement, joined in "Come on love, sit down."

Hannah did as she was told and quickly turned her venom on Tim "not seen you since you left..... what was it twenty years ago?"

"Yeah, look sorry about that."

"No you're not."

"I really am."

Mrs MacKenzie's phone rang, and she took the call. Hannah lowered her voice and in a raspy, hushed and threatening tone said,

“One call to our Steven and you’d both be dead. But you’re not going to be that lucky. Only lucky people get to die.”

“Look Hannah I’m sorry," said Tim “I wish I could turn back time, act differently, make it up to you I really do.”

Hannah’s face turned suddenly mellow and the jovial tone of their schooldays returned to her voice as she asked for Tim’s number. Reluctantly he sang out the digits before exchanging the obligatory first text to make sure they had entered them correctly. Tim saved the number under the contact name “crazy Hannah Mack (Gy)” which Karl read over his shoulder forcing him to splutter tea through his nostrils. He and Tim had a lot of catching up to do and a few truths to be ironed out he thought.

In the taxi on the way home Mrs MacKenzie smiled and commented how nice it was to have her old daughter back and it was amazing what seeing her friends had done. Hannah was oblivious to this as she text Tim to ask him when he was taking her out on a date.

Δ Δ Δ

The White boys sat either side of Bobby's space in the Jube as they toasted their father. It seemed ironic to do so in a manner that had brought this situation to being but they couldn't think of a better way. Karl rose to buy another round as Tim took his last mouthful and watched the bubbles of lacing descend the glass.

"No mistaking whose son he is," Steve said from his perch at the bar "he was proud of you both you know, these are on me."

As Karl returned with two beers Tim had a very furrowed brow.

"Free beer off Paedo Steve. What's up with your face?"

"Five fucking times"

"What?"

"That's how many times she's text the same message since I last looked at my phone! The same message look," - he held the screen to his brother.

"Fucking hell,"

"I knew she had problems, but she's fucking tapped,"

"Absolutely but still got great tits,"

"What do I do?"

"Great tits Tim, great tits. Anyway what's the score with you and her,"

Tim started at the beginning and told his version of events before spinning back to the conversation he'd had with Gemma about the abortion. Karl's countenance turned ashen - whiter than a sheet - as he recalled the one time he and Hannah shagged and remembering the conversation about her being on the pill so not needing a Johnny vividly.

"Fuck man,"

"I already worked out it was yours,"

"So what? You gonna take her out,"

"I reckon I can stall till Dad's funeral then fuck knows,"

"You going back to Manc after we bury him?"

"I've no idea, I've always fancied a little beach bar somewhere;"

"Well it's not like you've got to work,"

"You're right but I would there, maybe one day you'll wake up and I'll be gone, fucked off to some tropical paradise selling cocktails,"

Tim's phone beeped

"Jesus, she says she's always loved me and would do anything for me."

# Chapter 40

They'd seen him before, they even could be classed as acquaintances, but they hadn't really paid much attention. Today seeing him at the hospital, he was clearly sensitive and emotional. Not like all the fucking slags and big headed men they'd fucked in the past. They'd followed him and his brother home from the hospital but they'd stuck together and there hadn't been any opportunity, but they would get him alone and they just had to have him. This one was different though so he might get treated to some lube and not so rough when the time came. And it would come - Oh yes it would.

Following him from a distance the next few days had been difficult. Always surrounded by family and people coming and going out of the house and lots of flower deliveries, but the time would come.

Tonight was the night. Unbeknown of his forthcoming fate he had left the house to go for a walk to clear his head before bed. He chose to take the "black path" route through the middle of the estate. Seizing the opportunity he was hit on the back of the head by a police issue cosh which sent him to his knees. He'd had his trousers pulled down and his anus lubed but they waited, they wanted him to be awake. It was getting dark but they waited. He let out a groggy sound as he regained semi-consciousness followed by a loud grunt as he took the cock deep in his virgin arse. The sensitive nature was nowhere near the thrill of the struggling and forced instances of the past. Another two blows to the back with the cosh and an increase of tempo and ferocity made his screams louder and more pained and much more enjoyable. Placing a gloved hand over his mouth they gyrated like a savage beast until their orgasm surged through their body. Giving a final blow with the cosh for good measures knocking him unconscious once more.

# Chapter 41

Tim's phone rang for the seventeenth time and he eventually opened his eyes to see who was ringing. It was Hannah. She'd been a bit full on since getting his number and now she was ringing at this time of night. He ignored it and flicked the switch to silent contemplating switching to Airplane mode. He reasoned that ignoring the calls and claiming sleep was a much better resolution than dealing with the consequences of blatantly diverting them to voicemail. He checked his Facebook feed and was just about to flick his phone off and go back to sleep when a message came through. Voicemail from Hannah. "Jesus" he thought as he held the phone to his ear. Sobs, horrific, violent and terrifying sobs.

"You're.....the..... own.....lee...he..per.....son.....I can.....spee...he..eek to, please.....pick.....up..he...it.....was..heh...hor.....rib.....b ull.....I was. ...just.. he... walk.. ...king.. .he..he... ..was....there.....bal.....la...heh heh...clar.....va.....please.....Tim......please"

He had heard enough, he hung up and called her.

"I'm.....heh......so.....glad you....heh.....rang....ba...haaack" the sobs were continuing. Tim realised that these weren't crocodile tears or an otherwise elaborate attempt to guilt trip him. These were genuine tears and Hannah was scared.

"Where are you?"

"Sat....ne....hear....Saint....Jayhamses.....church.....I ......cahan't.....go.....home"

"Calm down and breathe, I'm on my way"

Tim hung up, he needed to get into town and he needed to do it quickly. He dialled the only local taxi numbers he could remember, 69s and 35s, but neither could sort him out. Going out into the cold of the night Tim's head was awash with thoughts yet bereft of ideas. He punched the gate in frustration and decided that his only option was to walk. Pacing down Wybers Way he noticed a very well maintained old Mini Cooper.

The car fired into life first time, the muscle memory of a misspent youth coming into play. Reversing off the drive, Tim exited the estate travelling the wrong way down the little dual carriageway. Not stopping at the red light the Mini's wheels squealing as he turned up Great Coates Road, barely keeping in control. Taking his phone out of his pocket he text Hannah.

Go near the White Hart, I'm in a green Mini

The tyres squeaked as he careened off Deansgate. Tim saw a very forlorn and ashen looking Hannah pacing up and down outside the pub. Screeching to a halt he opened the passenger side door and Hannah's face softened with relief. She leant over and hugged Tim, hot salty tears rolling down her cheeks as she just repeated "it was horrible" over and over. Tim bear hugged her and patted her back.

"You're safe now" he reassured her.

Driving away from town to the relative safety of the seafront Hannah broke down as she told the chain of events. She'd had an argument with her Mum and stormed out of the house. It was gone midnight. It wasn't raining but she had her hood up for its comforting nature of blocking out the outside world. She'd walked and walked and walked and had ended up in People's Park. She'd done six circuits of the lake when she felt a presence behind her. Turning round she'd seen a man in a balaclava raising his fist. His eyes were glazed over but had widened when he saw her face and he ran off.

"We need to go to the police Han"

"We can't"

"Why not?"

"They already think it's Steven and they'll ask why he's ran off and I'm the first one to be left alone"

"No they won't"

"They will, you don't know what this Morris is like. The thing is though Tim, he WAS exactly the same size as our Ste"

The conversation was abruptly halted by a phone call - Karl.

"I don't know what the fucks just happened, well I think I do, I do know I.....I don't wanna say it but mate I need your help"

# Chapter 42

Tim was angry. Really fucking angry. His best mate, his brother and his (whatever the fuck Hannah was) friend all attacked by this monster within a week of each other. He vowed revenge. He moved himself, Hannah and Karl into the chalet he had bought on the Fitties when he first won his money. He had bought it "just in case" and had somewhat forgotten about it. He'd never imagined what one of these "just in case" moments would be and he'd not envisioned this. The chalet was cosy and in dire need of some DIY but it provided them all somewhere to feel safe whilst Tim planned his vengeance.

Tim had bought an old banger and was driving it unregistered, untaxed, well overdue its latest MOT and on a pair of false plates- the V5 in the post to a made-up name and address. It was a rusty death trap but he was only really driving in it at night and not while the roads were busy. He'd been out every night for three weeks, driving aimlessly around Grimsby and Cleethorpes, following girls walking on their own, probably frightening the hell out of them and running the risk of becoming a suspect himself. It was the twenty-fourth night on the trot he had done this same route around the town. His final stop in Cleethorpes was Sidney Park. Checking all the bushes with his torch he walked around and around, remembering how exciting it was as a child seeing the whale bones there. Nothing there again tonight just an old drunkard and his cider. It was usually in Sidney Park he'd get despondent about his fruitless, and frankly futile searching, but it's all he could do. He got back in his car and drove down Durban Road, pulling off Welholme Road onto Park Drive and killing the engine. He got out and walked towards where the aviary was. The fountain in the lake was making a hissing sound and making him need a piss. He carried on walking round to the kids play area, checking as many bushes as he could, all the time the fountain's sounds playing havoc with his bladder. He carried on past the bandstand as he continued checking the outside of a copse of trees but once again to no avail.

Trying to be as inconspicuous as possible, he entered the copse took out his cock and felt intense relief as he unloaded a huge steam of piss that would have made a racehorse proud. As he fastened himself up he turned round to be face to face with a man in a balaclava.

He saw red; a crimson mist descended; he didn't even hear them say his name as he swung a right fist at them. They grabbed it and followed with a right of their own, glancing Tim's temple. A right boot to the stomach from Tim caused them to bend over and was followed by a knee narrowly missing their balaclava enclosed face. Composing themselves before the right hand hit the back of their head a quick jab to Tim's ribs was followed by a shoulder charge which sent both tumbling to the ground. The attacker recuperated first and stumbled over, straddling Tim's chest and beginning to choke him with gloved hands. Tim feeling the oxygen leaving his body began to see black - passing out as the rapist squeezed tighter. His arms scrambling around to try and pull the hands from his throat. He found a large branch on the floor which he swung with all of his remaining might into the side of the attacker's head. Once, twice, three times as eventually the vice around his throat eased and he could wrestle this guy off him. Another blow to the cheek area with the branch left them prone. A fog of vermillion and scarlet and every other hue of red imaginable descended on Tim as he straddled the balaclava'd figure.

# Chapter 43

"Right gather round please,"

Vikki knew it was serious if Amir, the main consultant, was giving a talk before the patient had even arrived. He continued to say that the ambulance had had an anonymous call to someone in a park and the paramedics had called to say they were in a bad way. The staff should prepare themselves for some shocking sights and anyone who wasn't up to it should step to one side. Vikki felt a pang of excitement. She loved patients like this, almost too much; it was why she'd stayed on A&E and turned down the opportunity for promotion to the elderly medicine ward. Her adrenaline surged as they got the call to say the ambulance was on Scartho Road. One minute until show-time.

They wheeled the wheezing carcass into the room. It's face no longer recognisable as human. Blood bubbled from where the nose should have been on the slab of tenderised meat attached to a contorted body. They quickly intubated via a tracheostomy to allow oxygen into his system, although where its brain used to lie in amongst all the mangle of flesh was anyone's guess. Vikki trying her hardest to administer painkillers to make them more comfortable, watching the heart monitor the room knew there wasn't long left.

BEEEEEEEEEEP

"Clear!"

"Up to 250 Joules, Clear!"

"Right are we all agreed? Time of death 4:27, let's leave it to the police now, good work everybody."

∆ ∆ ∆

PC Knight was nearly sick as he looked under the covers at the badly beaten body of the deceased, much to the amusement of PC Anderson.

"Fuck me that is some kicking" he exclaimed as his colleague went through the possessions for clues as to who was lying there. Rifling through the wallet he took a sharp intake of breath as he dropped it on the floor. He radioed through and asked for DCI Morris.

"Sir, it's about Steve MacKenzie"

# Chapter 44

Time

.

.

.

.

.

stood

.

.

.

.

.

still.

# Chapter 45

It might have been seconds. It may have been an hour. It was probably more like a couple of minutes. The twisted reality and blind rage Tim had been experiencing lifted as he threw the last of his broken knuckles into the lifeless corpse between his legs. He took a deep inhale and held it for as long as possible as clarity found its way back into his previously disassociated mind. He stood up and looked down at what he had done. This bastard had raped Karl, and he had said he would kill them if he caught him, but he was just speaking figuratively, but here they was he'd literally killed him. He looked at his shaking hands, knuckles swollen and distorted, covered in someone else's blood. A fear gripped his stomach, and a vice tightened around his chest as he spewed bile out into the base of a nearby tree. Struggling to breathe, his nostrils on fire, he was sick again and for a third time. Wiping the blood off his hands on a patch of grass, he fumbled into his pocket for his fags and lighter. Picking a bent cigarette out from the crumpled packet Tim held it to his lips and eventually managed to get a flame between his trembling hands. Taking deep pulls he felt the easing benefits of the nicotine as he decided what the hell to do. Lighting another bent fag from the stub of the other he rang Karl.

"Mate I need some help here,"

"What? What the fuck? You get him?"

"Yeah, I just need some help,"

"Where are you?"

"Peoples Park. Don't tell Hannah;"

"Yeah yeah ok, what do you need,"

"A van and some bin bags. There's an old carpet in the shed. Bring that too,"

"Where the fuck am I gonna get a van from?"

"You're a resourceful guy, figure it out!"

"Ok mate. See you later."

Tim hung up. Still buzzing from the fight yet petrified from the corpse, he wanted to run but knew he had to dispose of this body. Too many people might have seen him tonight.

Δ Δ Δ

A quick flick of the screwdriver and the door opened. It fucking stank. Just Karl's luck at the moment that the only van he could find was a fish round van. He pulled out his old transponder key bypass kit and closed his eyes, praying to a God he'd long given up on that it would work and that Tim was ok. The fourth key turned and the engine came to life. Carefully reversing off the drive Karl's heart was fluttering as he made his way back to the chalet to pick up the stuff Tim had requested before heading towards Peoples Park.

"It's a fucking fish van; but it's a van" Karl shouted down the phone, nerves on edge as he sped down North Sea Lane.

"That might be just as well, might need the refrigeration"

Δ Δ Δ

The White brothers embraced at the edge of the park as Tim led the way to the still body.

"Why didn't you take the balaclava off?"
"I don't want to see his face."
"I fucking do."
"Not while I'm about you don't."

Karl gave the corpse a few kicks in frustration and retribution for his ordeal, Tim having to hold him back. They struggled to roll the body into the carpet and then covered it loosely in thick black garden waste bags and lifted one end each, labouring across the open space to the parked van before dumping the body in the back.

"Heavier than they look." Tim remarked.
"Like a dead weight." Karl half joked.
"Sick cunt! We've got to get rid of him though."
"I know, any ideas?"
"Not yet but Ben needs to know too."

# Chapter 46

Away from the glare of the orange sodium street lamps Craig paced up and down awaiting the mysterious man to appear and give him his final instalment of payment. He'd felt bad enough doing a mate over for two-and-a-half grand but he sure as hell wanted the remaining half. It wasn't just being scammed out of twelve hundred and fifty notes he was concerned about either, they'd reneged on their side of the deal and what was meant to be a roughing up now left him facing a murder, or at best manslaughter, charge - all for a paltry sum of money.

It had all gone so well and to plan at first. Acting drunk and being a bit of a mouthy bastard, beating Macca at pool then darts, deliberately spilling his drink on Macca's trainers, then his pièce de résistance of hitting Macca's drink out of his hand with a pool cue and offering him outside for a fight. Calling him a puffter might have taken it too far, but he saw the rage as Macca's eyes narrowed to murderous slits. It wasn't difficult to lure him into the park either, walking backwards - arms out, hands beckoning, "come on then you cunt". Macca playing the stalking predator to aplomb straight into the ambush this guy had set up.

Not hanging around to watch after hearing the first sickening thud of a baseball bat against his skull, Craig simply returned to the pub and finished his pint. The hero's welcome and the drinks which the clientele proffered him had pacified him. Reasoning that Macca was a cunt and had hurt so many people over the years that he probably had it coming to him eventually. But he couldn't quite get his head around why they'd gone so far as to kill the bastard - and why had they had to get him involved? Especially with it all being so covert.

Eventually the man turned up, a trilby hat pulled down covering his face like something out of a 1920's American detective movie. He handed over a brown envelope, thickened full of used ten pound notes. Craig had insisted on this, not because of any reason other than he'd heard it in films and he felt the first conversation had needed some mirth adding and he thought it would make him sound more professional. Slipping it into the inside pocket of his jacket Craig noticed the guy's face for the first time as he took a pull on his cigarette and it was illuminated by the orange cherry at the end. He recognised him but couldn't quite place him. He'd thought it was off the telly but why would someone like that be getting involved with Macca?

"You did well" the man spoke breaking the obstinate silence albeit briefly before taking another draw on his cigarette, once again partially irradiating his angular features - "do not worry about the police."

Thoughts rushed into Craig's head like the start of the Grand National - "The police - that's where I know the guy from! He's the face you see at the press conference whenever there's been one of those beast rapes - the guy in charge!" - "bu.... but why kill him?" He manages to brave up to say - "Some questions are best left unanswered but let's just say the world is a better place without him" and with that the man in the hat egressed leaving Craig alone with more thoughts.

∆ ∆ ∆

As he threw the trilby onto the passenger seat he suddenly was gripped with a fear. This guy, this Craig, wasn't really up to the job of keeping his mouth shut and his eyes had widened in recognition just then - he couldn't allow that to happen.
He knew full well that Craig still ran with the football mob so Morris picked up his iPhone and checked the fixture list. It was time to call in a favour from a friend on another force and make sure that Craig suffered a similar fate to MacKenzie at the hands of an opposing firm. He dialled the number.

# Chapter 47

Tossing and turning, covered in a layer of sweat, images of balaclavaed figures injecting heroin up his arse flashing through his brain. Ben wasn't awake, but he certainly wasn't asleep. He hadn't slept properly since the attack and the burning want for smack was getting worse. Vikki had helped talk him through but her words were scant comfort compared to what the warmth of a hit would give him. He got out of bed and went to the toilet, looking at his bloodshot eyes in the mirror, sunken like two pissholes in the snow. He'd give anything for that shot and the inevitable sleep that would enable. Grabbing a dirty pair of jeans and a top from the wash basket, he decided he needed to go out and find his relief.

Walking towards the door his stomach tightened, knotting like a fist. His heart pounded in his chest as he turned the key and his chest tightened as the outside air, not felt since the attack, hit his lungs. He collapsed, gasping for air like a fish who'd jumped out of its tank. Paralysed with fear he lay there waiting.

Vikki had woken when she heard the door and was scared when she didn't feel Ben next to hear in bed. She knew he hadn't been sleeping, and he'd become withdrawn, not venturing out of the house. She feared the worst when she realised he'd gone out now. Getting up to get a drink she noticed the front door ajar, cursing Ben she went to close it and saw him lying prostrate in the front garden crying.

"Come on baby, come inside" she said placing a reassuring hand on his back, rubbing with a gentle vigour "Come on."

She made a strong cup of tea, placing three sugars in it and fed it to him. Ben slowly returning to a state in which he could speak.

"I'm sorry, I just need to feel safe."

The phone rang. Tim with the news.

"You going to be ok?"

"I am now"

Δ Δ Δ

They were greeted by a pale looking Tim as they pulled up outside the chalet. He ushered them round to the shed. As they walked in Vikki and Ben saw a roll of carpet lying on a wallpaper pasting table.

"They in there?" Ben asked violently.

"Yes mate."

"Who the fuck is it?"

"Dunno, I don't wanna see their face. I'll let you and Karl do it when I'm not here."

"Where is Karl?"

"Just sorting something out, he'll be back soon."

Ben walked up to the table and punched the corpse hard, grazing his knuckles on the hessian back of the carpet.

"Cunt!"

∆ ∆ ∆

They sat in silence drinking Laphroaig whisky out of mugs. The peaty flavour unappetising to Vikki but the warmth and relaxing qualities of the alcohol much welcoming. A fraught looking Karl walked in, smelling of petrol and smoke, he poured a large measure of the Scotch and necked it in one foul gulp. The atmosphere icy, not one of old friends meeting in happy circumstances, nobody daring to mention the proverbial elephant in the room, which in this case was a dead body wrapped in black bags and a carpet in the shed.

"We need to think," Tim broke the deathly silence "we need to dispose of that thing."

"How?"

"Weigh it down and dump it in the docks?"

"Too risky, could be seen."

"I think we need to separate it up."

"Good plan. How?"

"I've got a chainsaw."

“Can we see who it is now?”

Tim left the shed, he was fighting enough with his conscience about killing someone without seeing their face. If it was up to him they’d never know but Karl and Ben needed understandable closure. He lit a cigarette and paced the garden. A loud gasp was followed by the sound of Vikki being sick and then shouting “you fucking bitch”. A thousand scenarios had played through Tim’s head but not a single one of them would involve the word bitch. Curiosity getting the better of him he re-entered the shed to see Ben restraining Vikki who was shouting “bitch” repeatedly. He looked at the table to see the battered face of Vikki’s workmate Jenny staring back at him.

∆ ∆ ∆

This was more difficult than he’d imagined. After never studying anatomy or butchery Tim didn’t quite know where to cut or at which angles as he mutilated Jenny’s joints to separate the body into manageable chunks. The legs proving the most troublesome as he separated the femur from the hip joint. The shed’s air pungent with a smell he'd never smelt before and never wished to smell again.

He now had twelve bags containing hands, upper and lower arms, upper and lower legs and feet, all that remained was to take off her head and then decide the best course of action to remove the viscera with as little mess as possible. He positioned himself to cut the neck, started the chainsaw and lowered it. He was stopped by a blood-curdling scream. Hannah stood at the door, white as a sheet, not quite believing her eyes.

"Err Hannah, you.....err.....wasn't meant to get involved in this."

∆ ∆ ∆

**VIKKI** - It feels like every pair of eyes in the hospital has been watching me today. I can't get a moment to myself to escape and get the bag out of my car. Everyone asking me if I've heard off Jenny because it's unusual for her not to phone in if she's sick. I feel myself going red every time someone mentions her name - then the anger hits me and I want to scream about what a bitch she is and if only they all knew what she was really like. I stay composed – I have to for Ben. She's already destroyed enough of his life without me compounding a prison sentence to it.

Feigning a cigarette break I get the bags and make my way to the operating theatres via the back entrance, keeping my face down so that nobody notices I'm not in the right department. I eventually find the yellow plastic bin where I can dispose of her and get that bitch sent for incineration.

**KARL** - I give Martin a call. I fully expect the backlash I receive because I've not spoken to him for months, maybe even a year. And yes, now I am contacting him because I need a favour. But that's what mates do for each other. Within 5 minutes of talking together it'll be like nothing's changed and we're 15/16 again. Except things have changed. Everything can never be the same. Things have really gone a-fucking-wry for me. I try my hardest to open up and tell him but the words stick in my throat, my voice box drys and cramps up and nothing comes. He breaks the silence by telling me his own problems with his ex-wife and custody of the kids, so by this point I decide the burden of my issues sure as hell will not help him either. I just explain I've got a favour to ask of him and can he help me out.

"Anything for my oldest mate" comes the reply and I'm glad. No real questions asked. I don't need to tell him why I need him to leave his Dad's butchers shop open overnight I just reassure him that it's nothing overly dodgy, I'm not robbing him and that he nor his Dad will get into shit for it - God I hope I'm right about that bit. I really do.

So here I am, it's 3 in the morning and I've got a bag full of viscera and crudely butchered leg muscles on the passenger seat. It fucking stinks and it's making me dry boke every time the smell wafts over to my nostrils. If you've ever opened a packet of supermarket pork past it's sell by date, then imagine that and multiply it by ten - then try to picture that the pork had raped you and your elder brother was in charge of the abattoir. I bet you'd be sick too.

Under the cover of darkness I'm round the back of the butchers and (true to his word - I knew I could rely on him) Martin has left the fire door open. I haven't got a clue what I will do next. Tim suggested there would be a bin full of giblets but if there is I can't see one in the dark. I clatter into a metal trolley full of hooks which echoes and reverberates around the empty shop. I make my way to the front retail section and there it is on the work surface - shining like a beacon - a lightning bolt strikes with an idea as I see it - the mincer.

It takes me a while fumbling in the dark to find the switches and make sure it's plugged in but I eventually get it going as I feed the insides of this bitch through the grinding machine and she extrudes out through the head at the front. Tight worms of greyish pink rapist offal spew through as I gather it back in the bag and begin another search for somewhere to dispose of the mince.

The storage fridge door is heavier than I anticipated and an icy cold blast emanates from it as I pull it open. There are rows of metal shelves down either side. On one of the shelves there is a large white plastic container marked "Lincs Mix" which when opened resembles a herbed and spiced version of what I have in my bag. Martin's Dad's award winning Lincolnshire bangers no doubt - a fresh batch ready to be put in their skins for the weekend rush. I tip the contents of the bag on top and massage it all together using my hands.

**TIM** - The rucksack containing her head and several bricks is on Ben's lap. I feel bad that it's him who has to do this but he insisted on helping and I wasn't going to turn him down - I don't think I could have done this bit alone. I'm sticking to the speed limit much to the annoyance of the guy behind us. We can see the bridge in the distance as we pull over the hill. We both shout "bridge" at the same time in an age old game which takes us back to being kids. The mirth we take from this alleviating the gravitas of the situation which we've found ourselves in. As I drive past the airport I find my mind wandering as I think about whether a plane has a transponder key like a car, so much so I nearly plough into a roundabout that wasn't there last time I drove this route. Ben starts laughing - giggling like a schoolgirl as he pulls out a joint and lights it. He passes it over to me and at first I decline but he insists that it'll calm my nerves so I take a deep hit. The stolen car fills with sweet smelling blue smoke as we continue our journey.

As we incline on to the Humber Bridge Ben inexplicably opens the bag - "fucking bitch" he screams at her long dead face before zipping the bag back up and opening the window ready for the next part of the plan. As we pass under the first huge pillar Ben starts with what I think is a strange tic - "nnnnnnnn". It takes me a good ten seconds to realise he is mimicking another game from our childhood as the shape of the suspension wire indicates we're getting close to the middle of the bridge. I join in "nnnnnnnn".

"NOW" we say in unison as Ben throws the rucksack out of the speeding car.

"FUCK SHIT BOLLOCKS!" He shouts as I look in the wing mirror to see the rucksack bouncing down the road not even making it to the pedestrian walkway.

"Fuck" I repeat as I slow down - BEEEEEP goes the wagon behind us. I step on the accelerator careening off and only just stopping in time for the toll booth. Ben jumps out and runs back down the path. I wheel spin away and get to the viewpoint as quickly as I can and dump the car. I run up just in time to see Ben in the distance and a rucksack falling to the brown murky water below, hopefully getting sucked down by the reeds to never be seen again. He is redder than a baboon's arse when I get to him, sweat dripping from his brow and still struggling to breathe as we collapse on the side of the bridge giggling at each other.

**HANNAH** - If you'd have asked me when I was a teenager, before all my problems started I'd have told you this was impossible. I was young and naive and probably very stupid no matter how big and clever I thought I was. But now as I sit listening to their laughter I know it's true, and it disgusts me. So yes, it's possible to love and detest somebody at the same time.

I've loved him since the first time we kissed. I just knew it was love. I may have been too young but it was more than lust, more than infatuation, it was bona fide love - still is, always has been and always will be. But it hurts so much now. The pain yet the numbness. I'd just found out about Steven getting murdered and needed someone, I needed my love, I needed a hug. The utter shock of walking in to the shed and seeing him there will stay with me forever. My Tim - his face distorted, maniacally, almost like he was enjoying butchering her head off with the chainsaw.

And I see them all, getting closer. Their bonds tightening. I know they're talking about me behind my back yet not paying any attention to me to my face. I need their help more than ever. I want to shout in their faces and tell them that I think they're scum but I can't - despite it all I love Tim too much. I need a hug from him, I need a hug from Steven but I can't. My love is not who I thought and my precious brother dead. Murdered yet the police seem indifferent. I know he wasn't an angel but nobody deserves what he has had done and it's almost as if the coppers know but don't seem it worth their effort - just one less scumbag to them but to me he was my fucking brother, my flesh, my blood.

Every time I close my eyes I see either Tim's twisted face with the chainsaw or Steven. It's impossible to breathe away, and it's impossible to sleep.

I wipe the tears from my face as I finish packing the bag and leave the chalet to go back to my Mums - I need my family and I doubt these bastards will even notice I'm gone. I doubt anyone would notice if I disappeared.

**BEN** - It's fairly safe to say I've been shitting myself waiting for the coppers to knock on since I fucked up throwing the bag on the bridge - what with all the CCTV around nowadays I think it's only a matter of time. I don't know what happened - I think the handle got wrapped around my wrist or something. I would say lesson learned but I have no intention of throwing a severed head in a rucksack out of a moving vehicle ever again.

With Vikki disposing of the hands and feet and Karl getting rid of Jenny's insides there's only really the ribs, spine and the arms and legs left in the shed. Granted these are quite a big thing to get rid of and would carry a lengthy sentence for us all if we got caught but Tim seems calculated. It scares me how duck-to-water easily he's taken to disposing of a body and I can tell it scares Hannah too.

On the plus side I've only thought of junk once since Jenny was killed - and that was when we had Chinese and Karl made a sick joke about the spare ribs we were eating. I needed and craved the escape but now I'm settled and almost back to normal, well as normal as someone with an old smack habit getting rid of a dead body with his friends can be - which to be frank isn't very conventional.

Tim bounds in and tells us of a friend of a friend from uni who lives in Mablethorpe. This guy has got a boat we can borrow if we want to go sea fishing - apparently he once caught a six foot tope (which looks like a shark) in the North Sea. Now despite what you might believe about people from Grimsby we aren't all born with fishing rods as an appendage and as far as I know the White brothers are similar to me as in they've never done a days fishing in their lives. My confusion is mirrored on Karl's face until the dawn of realisation hits us both at the same time.

As we load up the car I can't help but realise we're an arm and a leg short - "Tim?" I enquire before he replies "Tetney Lock and the docks mate" without the actual question needed to be asked.

The last of the femurs makes a big splash into the waves as Tim launches it with all his might, almost as big as the splashes from the contents of Karl's stomach. A green looking Karl wipes a chunk off his chin. Tim giggles inwardly before making a terrible pun about sea legs.

We're at Tetney before the colour eventually returns to Karl's face and the mood in us all has notably shifted. There is levity in our joking but our mirth is cut short by Vikki's seriousness.

"The job still isn't over" - she speaks with an icy tone. Her inflection more suited to a headmistress or parent to that of a friend and girlfriend.

**VIKKI** - I swear to God I feel like their bloody mother sometimes. I don't mind doing the odd bit of housework and tidying up after them but it's bloody ridiculous having to tell them off for behaving like children. I feel so mirthless because I can tell they're relieved but I've seen enough TV dramas to know it isn't over until it's over and that shed and this car need a bloody good clean before we're safely out of the woods. Then and only then will I feel like we can return to semi-normal and the levity and joviality can resume.

**KARL** - Can't believe I've ruined me best jeans with fucking bleach. The day at sea and losing the contents of my stomach meant I was starving by the time we got back and all I wanted was me tea but no, little Miss Vikki said we had to clean the shed out and I've ended up with splashes up the front. Fucking Stone Island too, a hundred and fifty notes. Ten or fifteen years ago I might have gotten away with it but not now - they look fucking ridiculous. I may as well burn em when I torch the car. Worse thing is I'm still famished - Hank fucking Marvin.

Tim's cooking, so all is not lost and he shouts us through to tell us it's ready. My stomach turns and I feel nauseous - sausages, chips and gravy.

"Where you get the bangers?" I ask - praying to God he doesn't say Martin's dads.

"Tescoses, Why?"

I explain the story about how I got rid of my share of Jenny and I feel sick again thinking about the poor cunts who have sat down to their tea expecting award winning Lincolnshire thick links. Tim pipes up something about human flesh tasting like pork anyway.

Vikki pipes up - "the cannibals call us longpigs."

“Great band,” Ben adds before singing “there’s no clothes I can buy make me feel like myself, She say-yeahd.”

“I’m surrounded by heathens” he adds as he sees the bewilderment on all three of our faces.

**HANNAH** - The buzz in my ears is getting louder and louder. I haven't slept. I can't sleep.

I don't want to.

Every time I close my eyes I see one of four things.

Steven with a demonic face.

Tim with a demonic face.

Jenny with a demonic face.

My beautiful Amber.

Amber was my daughter.

Our daughter.

Mine and Tim's,

sorry Karl's.

Beautiful before they made me so callously remove her.

I'm trying to keep awake.

I don't want to see any of that.

I eat coffee from the jar with a spoon.

The bitter taste worth it.

The buzzing gets louder.

So So

Loud

I hate it.

I hate them.

I

Hate

Myself

I

Want

To

Die

**TIM** - The smell of phosphorus hits my nostrils as I strike the match and genie the packet. I throw it towards the petrol soaked shed as the flames envelope the timber building, licking up the side. The blue paint starts to bubble before a canister inside explodes taking the full side off.

The noise has alerted the nosey Yorkie bastards in a nearby chalet so I start making a half arsed attempt with the hose pipe knowing full well it'll just dilute out the petrol, hoping it'll fuel the fire more because I need most of this shed gone before the brigade gets here - and they're on their way - the old couple take great delight in telling me.

The rest of the structure collapses just before we hear the sirens and Vikki is visibly relieved, her demeanour changing almost instantly.

"Job done" she says.

And I know it is, but I have a niggling doubt about Hannah's mental state. She's stopped replying to all our messages and I try to reassure Karl she's cool when he too voices concerns - I hope to God I'm right.

# Chapter 48

The intense burning on her arm from the cigarette she held there gave Hannah a brief moment of relief from her own thoughts. In that rare moment of purity she wrote down everything she needed to say to everyone she needed to say it to. She couldn't carry on, she was tired, she was exhausted, but most of all confused that everything she ever thought was wrong, everything she ever loved distorted, everything she thought she knew was a sham. She looked in the corner of the room. Her beautiful daughter, now 18, looked back at her and smiled. "See you soon Mummy" she said as Hannah lit another cigarette and let the hot cherry red end slowly burn on her wrist. Walking to the bathroom she washed down the remaining six of her venlafaxine tablets with a swig from the half empty vodka bottle before starting on the paracetamol boxes she had purchased earlier.

Catching a glimpse of herself she punched the mirror until it smashed then continued washing down the paracetamol with the vodka. She saw her Mum's warfarin in the cabinet - "rat poison" her Mum had called it. Why not? She thought as she took those for good measure before lowering herself in the hot bath water, immersing her face fully while frantically slashing at her arm with a razor blade. Eventually severing the radial artery turning the bath water pink as she drifted out of consciousness.

Δ Δ Δ

The phone rang and rang and rang. Lucas ignored it. It was his day off and he sure as hell didn't want it interrupting by an inane call off some uniform needing telling how to wipe their own arse. He reopened Grindr, back to the cute straight guy who was curious about getting his cock sucked. He sent him another message before the phone rang again.

"For fucks sake this better be good."

“It’s the youngest MacKenzie girl, she’s topped herself.”

“And?”

“And I think you’ll want to read the note.”

∆ ∆ ∆

If you’re reading this you meant something to me. Probably too much.

Mum, I’m sorry, I know you’ve only just lost Steven and I’m so fucking sorry to do this to you but I can’t go on. This was never your fault, please understand that. It has nothing to do with how you raised me. You were a great Mum to all of us, you did nothing wrong. It’s just the way I was wired.

Steven, I know you’re dead but I’m sorry. You were never the same after prison and the coppers thought you were the rapist. I even doubted you myself, I’m sorry. I know now it wasn’t you. I wish I didn’t find out the way I did but I’m sorry. I just hope the police catch the bastard.

Karl, my baby's daddy. I'm sorry I killed our baby, I'm sorry I only slept with you to get at Tim. I'm sorry you had to get involved.

Tim, I loved you, I still love you, I'm sorry Tim but I can't love a killer. Even if you killed a rapist I can't love you the way my heart wants to love you. Knowing you killed her with your bare hands I can't go on. The look on your face as you chainsawed her head off will be etched in my mind forever.

Im just sorry I couldn't be the person you all wanted me to be.

This is goodbye.

Don't cry for me,

my pain is over.

∆ ∆ ∆

Lucas held the tear splattered note in his hand, the writing disparate. Well thought out and neat in places yet scribbled and messy in others. His gaze concentrated on areas as he computed what he was reading

"I know now it wasn't you."
"Killed a rapist."
"Her."
"Tim."
"Tim"
"Tim......killed a rapist.....her."

He swore loudly as the realisation he and Morris may have been wrong all along hit him. He knew he had to find who Tim was and get him in for questioning. After all there was some suggestion here that there may be a murder to investigate.

# Chapter 49

A cooling breeze was coming in off the estuary as Tim leant against the metal railings of the promenade looking out towards Spurn lighthouse. The old war forts in the river glistening in the sun showing their brutalistic beauty. He looked left at the water lapping at the feet of the pier. Venue of many a drunken night out in its previous guise as a nightclub it was now a fish and chip restaurant of his mother's lament. She was, of course, correct in saying it was a shame it wasn't a local company like Steele's but to bemoan the fact they sold Hull style patties instead of "proper" fishcakes when she only ate fried fish was bordering on the ridiculous. Tim watched the Yorkie holiday makers, the grockles, the comforts (comfort' day) buzzing their way up and down the prom, eating their ice creams, their donuts, their fish and chips, feeding their faces before feeding the 2p slots and smiled to himself. It was tacky, but he loved the place, the clean air in his lungs, he missed the seaside the most. Even the beach looked clean nowadays although the chemical plants further down the river were still operational so he probably wouldn't brave the water. He lit a fag and watched some more, the images of the murder slowly leaving him as he remembered the relief in Karl and Ben's faces. It was, when all was said and done, self defence.

In his past he would have flicked the cigarette butt onto the beach, but a sense of civic pride made him stub it out and carry it towards a bin as he made his way towards the leisure centre to get a coffee at the kiosk. A group of children and lazy adults came past waving on the road train nearly knocking over a careless jogger too involved in their Fitbit reading to pay attention. Arriving at the kiosk he ordered a latte and sat outside in the glorious sunshine imagining a life back home. Of course he'd have to go back to Manchester at least once as he couldn't expect Ian to look after Mendonca the cat forever, besides he missed that bloody cat and his psychopathic tendencies.

∆ ∆ ∆

Lucas had been driving around idly for hours eventually ending up on the prom. The resort was packed and the pubs were dangerously over spilling. A boy racer in a Golf caught his attention as he sped past, very nearly taking his wing mirror off. Flicking on the lights he drives after him, ready to pull him in and give him a warning and nothing more - he couldn't be arsed with the paperwork. The Golf sped up away, sparks flying from it's lowered body as it hit the speed bump. Lucas depressed the accelerator as he sped after him down Kingsway. The Golf jumped over the mini roundabout with Queen's Parade, Lucas struggling to keep control of his BMW in pursuit as the headed towards King's Road, checking his mirror at the double roundabout Lucas slammed on the breaks screeching to a halt letting the Golf escape. He checked and checked again, it was definitely him. Leaving the car in the middle of the road to a queue of beeping traffic he began walking over towards the kiosk.

"Timothy White?"

∆ ∆ ∆

Tim watched the commotion unravel as he sipped his coffee, a screeching Golf followed by a BMW that came to an abrupt halt. He knew. His adrenaline pumping as the guy exited the car and walked towards him, his legs ready to go. The guy said his name, he pushed the table over and stood, sending the chair flying. He sprinted, jumping over the steps knocking into a woman with a Labrador before gathering his balance and running down the prom, woe betide any dawdling grockle who got in his path. He checked over his shoulder, he had about 20 yards on the copper. His lungs burnt as he upped the pace turning right onto the pier, up the ramp and down the side of the building as he hurdled the fence into the shallow water below.

∆ ∆ ∆

The helicopter hovered over the beach looking for signs of the accused. Lucas was certain he'd see him at the bottom drowning, legs broken, even crawling back to the beach but nothing.

No sign of him at his chalet on the Fitties, nothing at his Mum's and his brother Karl genuinely hadn't seen him since that morning (not that he'd have told the police otherwise). The colleagues over in Greater Manchester just found a well fed cat that had scratched the hell out of them and a friend who claimed to have been feeding the cat for two months and hadn't heard off him for over a week.

# Chapter 50

He straightened his tie in the mirror and ran a comb through his hair before taking a big gulp of vodka followed by mouthwash. Leaving the toilet and sitting back in the waiting area he wondered why the chief had called him in for a chat. He was called through.

"Look Luke, can I call you Luke?"

"I prefer Lucas."

"Ok Lucas, your colleagues are worried about you."

Nosy bastards thought Lucas, I'm absolutely fine - "why's that Sir?"

"They say you're becoming obsessed with finding this White character and they're worried you've become erratic."

"But I'm certain White holds the key Sir."

"The key to what?"

“Proving that there was 2 rapists, MacKenzie and the unnamed female.”

“And your colleagues are worried about your drinking, they say you’re out of control.”

“I’m fine Sir, just the odd pint after work” he lied.

“I think you need some time off, the service has plenty of help for you if you need it.”

“But Sir I’m fine.”

“Look after the garden Lucas, go fishing, just get better, you’re a good detective.”

# Epilogue

*"Fuck off" he says to me putting the phone down after I've used my best Indian call centre voice asking him if he wants to upgrade his internet speed. I want to scream, break the facade, tell him it's me and where I am but I can never do that, I can never go home. I look in the mirror, I have a healthy tan but my hair and beard are too long and you can see the grey hairs beginning to poke through. I really need to start trimming my nasal hair too. The non-prescription glasses accentuate the green in my eyes and I sometimes barely recognise myself when I've got them on. I step away from the mirror and look at my stomach, flatter than it's ever been before. A healthy diet, regular runs on the beach and a strict regime of no booze have seen to that. If I can only give up the fags, I'll be a happier man.*

*A woman who looks older than her years and always talks to me with an air of disdain like I owe her something is stood at the bar.*

*"Are you serving now?" She says to me like I'm something she's stepped in. She's clearly used this resort a long time, way before it became a playground for rich Russians with dubious backgrounds or a paedophilic paradise.*

*"Sorry love" I say to her in my recently acquired generic accent. Difficult to pinpoint - not quite Northern, not quite Southern but certainly no Midlands drawl. Her face distorts at my friendliness. "same again?"*

*I prepare her Piña colada while singing Rupert Holmes in my best off key voice.*

*If you like Piña coladas, getting caught in the rain. If you're not into yoga, if you have half a brain.*

# Acknowledgements

A special mention to Ants and Olivia - you were both inspirational and enthusiastic about this project and without your encouragement these pages would not exist.

Also gratitude to those on Dr. Graham Clingbine's book, author and reading group and the Writers in the Wood Facebook page (particularly Lorraine Reed and Steven J. Pemberton) - your help and encouragement has been second to none, this is also extended to Paula Geister and Melanie Hawthorne and members of numerous other Facebook groups.

Bill Price - you are a star for the artwork - I owe you more than a pint or two.

Lastly (and by all means most importantly) thank you to you, the reader, for reading this book and sticking with it right until the acknowledgements page!

If you would like to know more about me as an author then I have Facebook and WordPress (both as Robert A. Mitchell author). My WordPress includes a blog of the process of this book. I'd love to hear from people who stumbled upon this book without knowing me.

I intend on publishing a novella soon so please keep an eye out for that.

Printed in Great Britain
by Amazon